Advanced Dungeons & Dragons®

2nd Edition

Official Game Accessory

Rogues in Lankhmar

Credits

Design: "Uncle" Wes Nicholson
Editing: Steven Schend
Cover Painting: Larry Elmore
Interior Art: Scott Rosema and Jeffery Barker
Cartography: Diesel
Typography: Nancy J. Kerkstra
Acknowledgments: Ed Greenwood, Mike Whelan
Production: Paul Hanchette

Dedication: To Jennie, who puts up with the odd hours and midnight phone calls.

ISBN 0-88038-907-6

9461

Table of Contents

Purpose and Goals

Rogues in Lankhmar is the first of a new series of supplements that expand the information on the city of Lankhmar by particular districts. This initial product covers the southeastern corner of the city, the Plaza and Tenderloin Districts; the area is notorious for the rough-and-tumble reputation of its people and their businesses. Needless to say, there is no shortage of adventure here. . . .

In this book, your group of brave player characters will find many newly detailed places, and encounter new groups and individuals in the streets of Lankhmar. Some of the places and people can be friendly, even benign, while others prove to be inimical or downright dangerous. A few can even be both, depending on the player characters' words and actions. Regardless of the person or the location, all contain great adventure possibilities, some decidedly more than others.

The material in this book is designed specifically for use by the Dungeon Master. It contains background information that players and their characters should not know before learning it within the context of game play. Indeed, the purpose of the book is to let the player characters and the nonplayer characters develop as they discover the information. *If you are running a player character in a Lankhmar campaign, do not read past this page!* To continue reading this product will only spoil the thrill of discovery as your characters explore the city.

Most of the adventures and encounters provided in this book can be adapted to characters of any level and class. There are notes at the end of the book that help the Dungeon Master to change the adventures to suit any player characters' levels, classes, or even alignments.

However, there is no reason why any players or Dungeon Masters should not have a copy of this book for reference. After you have explored the parts of Lankhmar detailed in this book, it will be a handy reference for player character contacts and could still provide possible adventures for your characters in the future.

A Rules Overview of Lankhmar

There are a number of differences between Lankhmar campaigns and those run in other AD&D® game worlds. While a number of these alterations are merely cosmetic (such as human racial differences), others have far more impact. The most significant of these differences are in the area of magic.

Player Character Races

Unlike the majority of TSR's game worlds, elves and dwarves and other demihuman races are all but unknown on the world of Nehwon. Aside from races such as the Nehwon ghouls, all player characters are humans. Major nationalities are:

Eevanmarenseers are totally hairless humans from a land far to the east of Lankhmar; their odd appearance imposes a –1 penalty to Charisma on such characters.

Kleshites are a dark-skinned race from the jungles to the south of Lankhmar. Shorter and quicker than most humans, they gain a +1 bonus to initial Dexterity scores.

Mingols are a small, nomadic race with slight builds but good agility (+1 bonus to Dexterity scores, –1 penalty to Strength scores). The Land Mingols are great riders and bowmen, and the Sea Mingols are skilled sailors.

Northerners are fair-haired barbarians from the savage Northlands. Northerner PCs gain a +1 bonus to Strength scores, but their warrior mentality also gains them a –1 penalty to their Wisdom scores.

Character Class Restrictions

Most of the standard AD&D character classes are present in Lankhmar, but each is adapted to the world in some way or form.

Warriors: Fighters function normally, though metal armor is extremely rare, and plate armor is (with few exceptions) nonexistent here. Paladins are rare here, and those that do exist are considered mildly deranged. Rangers are rare in Lankhmar but are more common in the wilderness. Neither rangers nor paladins gain any spellcasting abilities at higher levels.

Rogues: Thieves are, by far, the most common character class in Lankhmar, the aptly-titled City of Thieves. Bards are also plentiful throughout Nehwon, though higher-level bards do not gain the ability to cast spells.

Magic in Lankhmar

Of the changes incurred on the AD&D game system in the Lankhmar campaigns, magic is the most affected area. Magic is a rare and dangerous power in the world of Nehwon and should always remain such. Refer to the core rules in the *City of Adventure* supplement for Lankhmar for more details, but the basic changes to magic are thus:

- Items of a magical nature are not common in Lankhmar. Due to rarity, a character's possession of even a simple magical item is likely to attract the attention of those who lives are driven by greed and ruled by violence.
- Spellcasters are separated into two groups: **white wizards**, which are the equivalents of normal AD&D clerics; and **black wizards**, which are the equivalents of normal AD&D wizards. Unlike their counterparts, white wizards have full access to all 16 spheres of priest spells, and black wizards have full access to all eight schools of wizard spells.
- Due to the god Death, *raise dead* and *resurrection* spells do not function in Nehwon; *wish* spells cannot bring someone back to life. Spirits of the dead travel to the Shadowlands, and a rare few have ever returned from death.
- Casting times for spells are always one time unit higher than those listed in the *Player's Handbook*. Thus, a spell with a casting time of one segment now requires one round, while a spell requiring several hours now needs several days to cast. Similarly, spells are regained much more slowly than in other worlds. All spells take a full week to be regained.
- Finally, in terms of spellcasting, black wizards pay a high price for their power. For each level beyond 5th level, the wizard gains a slight deformity as the cost for wielding such power.

Role-Playing Guidelines

This book mostly details people and places that are well established in Lankhmar, and most civilized citizens do not solve their problems with blades and brawn. Simply hacking away at anything that annoys you is not only counter-productive, it will easily get the player characters jailed or even killed. This reduction of combat, combined with the scarcity of magical items, can slow down the advancement of player characters' experience points and levels to the point where players become disinterested in the campaign. The shortage of experience points won by combat and treasure acquisition can be offset by awarding more experience for roleplaying.

A successful exercise in diplomatically solving a confrontation should be rewarded just as much as a successful combat. Even an unsuccessful attempt at a peaceful solution to a problem should be rewarded, provided the attempt was genuine.

Pay particular attention to the social levels of the characters and their notoriety within the city. Fafhrd and the Gray Mouser should be used as plot devices by the DM, to keep a party on the right track, or to help them out in difficult situations. Be careful not to have the heroes pop up too often or the players will come to expect that their characters can do anything, no matter how suicidal, and they will be rescued in the nick of time.

Finally, even if your campaign is not based in Lankhmar, the establishments and people detailed in this book can be readily adapted to any fantasy world.

CHAPTER 1

Groups & Guilds in Lankhmar

Bargew's Traveling Circus

Plaza District

Bargew's circus travels the lands of Nehwon, but rarely stops for long lest they wear out their welcome. Wherever they travel, crime increases during their stay, but authorities assume that thieves are attracted by the crowds and the dwellings left vacant while the owners are at the circus. No one thinks that the circus might be the culprits.

Once a year, the circus comes to Lankhmar for five days of performances. There are two performances each day, one in the afternoon and one in the early evening. Admission to either show is one smerduk for an adult and one agol for an accompanied child.

When the circus is in Lankhmar, it sets up either in the Plaza at the fountain end, or where the DM places Marketplace Geomorph B or Open Field Geomorph (see the *City of Adventure* book). The circus always sets up in the Plaza District, avoiding the other entertainments of Festival District. If the circus is run in the Plaza, many regular traders take a vacation, whether on their own initiative or because they are "invited" to do so by the circus people. No one refuses an "invitation" from Bargew's Circus, as animals often "accidentally" escape near vendors who don't cooperate.

Bargew is the owner and ringmaster of the circus. He is a portly gentleman with a ruddy complexion and a genial manner. He is about 50 years old, but appears closer to 40 unless scrutinized closely. Bargew is an expert at disguises. Bargew is also a fence, dealing in jewelry and objets d'art. He will buy any item, no matter how hot it is, but his prices are based on how long he will have to keep an item before he sells it. Traveling as much as he does, it is simple for Bargew to buy an item in Horborixen and sell it six months later in Lankhmar. Although the prices he pays are affected by an item's risks, Bargew always sells the items at a fair price, keeping in mind the uniqueness of the items he trades in.

Maretta is Bargew's wife of 27 years. She is a few years younger than her husband, and is quite attractive. She is slim, and stands a full head above Bargew. Her raven hair shows no sign of graying, and her emerald eyes miss little that goes on around her. She is the circus' lion tamer, and she fearlessly steps into the cage with her three lions twice a day. What the public does not know is that these lions were bred in captivity and have never been taught to stalk their prey; they are also so well fed that they would never consider attacking Maretta.

Bargew and Maretta have two sons and three daughters, all of whom are married. They have eleven grandchildren from ages three to twelve. All five children and their spouses are performers in Bargew's Circus. Four of the grandchildren are now training seriously to perform in the circus.

The sons Guilio and Merko are trapeze artists. They swing on their trapezes high above the crowd, with no net beneath them. As they leap and swing, audience members crane their necks to see what's happening, and other circus folk use the chance to sneak under the seats and rifle through pouches.

Guilio's wife, Leesette, is a high-wire walker. She can traverse the wire with or without a balancing pole. Leesette always comes into the ring two acts after the trapeze artists. The timing lets her run over nearby rooftops to find prime targets, and return in time to tell her husband and brother-in-law which homes or buildings to raid. Her act also gives Guilio and Merko time to do the heists before the grand finale.

Merko's wife, Jessen, normally trains the dancing bears, but she currently is pregnant with her second child. She looks after the ticket office now, with the bears' training in the capable hands of her sister-in-law, Sarja.

Sarja is Bargew's and Maretta's oldest child, and she is a jack-of-all-trades. She is part clown, part sword-swallower, and part bear trainer. Sarja knows of the circus' other activities, but she is too busy keeping the audience distracted to join in any heists.

Sarja's husband, Bron, is the circus strongman. He is a Mingol who gave up raiding for a life of subtle plundering and greater profit. His physical prowess is excellent. He can lift a draft horse over his head, or easily pick up a 200 pound man in each arm. If there is trouble on the circus grounds, Bron also doubles as the circus bouncer. As such, the crisis is usually settled very quickly, and often brutally.

Bargew's second daughter, Jinni, is a trickrider. She rides into the ring on two matched gray horses, one foot on each horse, and she performs intricate maneuvers with the animals all around the big top.

Jinni's husband, Pegra, is the lead clown in the circus. He is the one who directs the comedy routines between main acts, keeping the audience occupied and entertained while props are removed or put in place. Although he is quite funny in the ring, he is quiet and sullen when out of his clown suit.

Merena, the youngest daughter, and her husband, Hafor, are also clowns. Hafor does the official books for the circus, the ones the tax collectors in the cities are shown. He also does the private books for Bargew, which show the circus' real revenues.

All the grandchildren get involved in the circus at the age of five. Before five, they are taught basic balancing and acrobatic skills while they play. At age five, they become ushers and snack vendors, hawking bags of roasted nuts in the stands between circus acts. At age ten, children are put to work in the box office, although Bron is never far away when the children are selling tickets (Bargew does not wish to be robbed).

Not all the circus performers are part of Bargew's family. Wenda the juggler joined the circus two years ago when she fled Quarmall due to a "misunderstanding" with the law. She is a gifted juggler and a passable gemsmith. Bargew has since added loose gems to his inventory, and has found he gets better prices on jewelry now. He pays Wenda a cut on all gem sales, but still makes more money than he did when he appraised the gems himself.

Other circus performers include Stefan the Eevanmarenseer fire-eater, and the Flying Hawks, a troupe of 14 acrobats who excel at human pyramids (and second-story work). All circus people are aware of the extra activities of the circus even if they don't take part directly. Everyone gets a cut, and their share depends on their involvement in the thefts or in keeping the locals busy.

Adventure Hooks

Bargew's Circus can be used simply to expand the background color of Lankhmar for a short period, allowing the PCs a change of pace from their usual entertainments. Should the PCs also learn of the circus' other works, there are many ways the PCs could have business with Bargew.

- They may have stolen something too hot to fence in Lankhmar, and be looking for a way out of their dilemma. If it fits one of the categories that Bargew deals in, he will pay them one quarter of its value—no questions asked. If it doesn't fit his needs, he will politely refuse to purchase the item, explaining that he is a circus operator, not a pawnbroker. He will never imply the item may be stolen.
- The party might have a price on their heads for some crime or offense against a powerful guild. If they have skills that could be useful in a circus, they may be taken on by Bargew as staff in exchange for help to get out of the city. Useful skills include high strength, high dexterity combined with at least a rudimentary knowledge of gymnastics, or thieving skills of an unusual type or at a high degree of expertise. Characters who do not possess these skills may be taken on as general attendants if Bargew can see a potential use for them or their comrades.
- For the more honorable PCs, they may be on the trail of a stolen object. Bargew's fencing operation is well known in thieves' circles, so it shouldn't be too hard to get on the trail. Getting the item back is another matter entirely. Bargew might sell it back to the PCs, as it doesn't matter to him who buys it. If they can steal it without getting caught, Bargew will accept the loss philosophically. However, if Bargew or any other circus member catches the PCs trying to steal something, there will be a battle. The PCs are unlikely to win due to sheer numbers, but Bargew would rather capture them alive if possible. The law will indenture them to him as slaves and he always needs people to muck out the animal wagons and haul firewood.

The Beggars' Guild

Plaza District

The Beggars' Guild is not really a group of down-and-out characters, as the name might suggest. Rather, they are an organized bunch of folk who don't want to work for a living. The beggars sit or stand on street corners each day with their begging bowls, hoping to pick up enough food or money to eke out an existence (or so people think). The number of beggars in an area at any time is controlled by the guildmaster, who lives off the tithes of his members.

Most folk simply ignore them, as beggars are a normal part of street life in Lankhmar. It is this anonymity in plain sight that is the guild's greatest asset. Guild members act as "galahs" for Thieves' Guild heists, and Assassins' Brotherhood jobs. A low whistle, a loud call of "alms for the poor," or hearty thanks to a generous patron can all convey a warning to the beggar's accomplices that trouble is coming. Naturally, the guild is paid well for this service. Payment goes directly to the guild; the beggar usually gets a 25% cut from the guildmaster later.

The prime spot for any beggar is the End Gate. Begging near this gate can net a beggar donations from all incoming travelers and merchants—especially those who don't want their presence or business in Lankhmar to be made public. Travelers who do not make generous contributions at this gate often find themselves the victims of "accidents," from broken cart wheels to personal injury. Everyone entering the End Gate is cased as a possible mark for later jobs by the Thieves' Guild. Again, payment for this service goes to the Beggars' Guild, not the individuals. They get only a 10% cut for this easy service.

The guild house is situated at the corner of End Gate Road and Beggars' Boulevard, just inside the End Gate. On the outside, it is simply a shabby two-story building. The first level is an open room with a makeshift counter where members pay their fees and pass on any news they hear in the streets. The guildsman at the counter also deals with any genuine beggars who enter. They are not treated kindly, and are removed as quickly as possible.

To keep up appearances, several members are always "asleep" around the room, keeping an eye on people from under their hoods. These "sleeping" members are actually the guards and they are armed with short swords under their tattered robes. Guards who truly fall asleep on duty are punished quite severely. It is the guards' job to keep nonmembers from going upstairs to the guildmaster's quarters. They also keep others from searching for the hidden cellar entrance on the main floor.

The top floor belies its shabby outward appearance, as it is quite comfortable and well maintained. It houses the guildmaster and the administration space for senior guild members. The guildmaster's suite looks out over the End Gate, while the senior members' offices overlook the surrounding streets. In the center of the top floor is a windowless room where guild planning takes place on a huge table with a city map on its top. This room is also used for interrogations and disciplinary hearings.

The guildmaster's suite has an attached strongroom with no walls adjacent to the outside of the building. The guild stores its collected fees and tithes for each week here. Once or twice a week, the bulk of the loot is removed to a secret location. This is done on random days, but usually happens every three or four days. Transfers to the guild's secret treasure hoard are never more than eight days apart.

The hidden cellar is a poorly kept secret in the guild. Many in the city have heard of it, but only guild members and some assassins and thieves have ever seen it and lived. Rumors abound about what it holds, from a secret sewer access to the location of the guild's wealth. Unlike most rumors, there is a little truth in them.

There is an entrance to the sewers known to few who live in the city, but those who dwell in Lankhmar Below know of it. There is also a small airtight vault in the cellar which occasionally holds guild loot, but not often—it isn't well protected against raids from below. The vault is used most often as an execution chamber, where rebellious members are locked up to slowly suffocate.

The cellar primarily serves as a brief hiding place for those on the run from the law. Up to thirty adults can comfortably fit into the cellar, and it has a number of small rooms along with one long communal bunk area. The smaller rooms are sometimes used for major meetings of the senior guild members or to gather beggars and thieves for a joint raid through the sewers.

While the city guards know the cellar exists, they do not know where its entrance is. Lankhmart law does not allow them to compel guild members to reveal its location. When an overzealous guard once tried to force a member to reveal the cellar, the beggar simply denied its existence. The guard was later found hanging by his ankles over the street on a lamppost. He was alive but severely beaten, and he swore he could not identify his attackers. Since this incident, no one in the city guard (or any other group) has tried to bully the cellar's location out of the guild.

Guild members who know the location of the secret cellar entrance can never leave the guild for another profession. Any members who attempt to leave are hunted down and killed before they can reveal any knowledge about the guild or the guild house's secret cellar. Even retirement is out of the question for a member of the Beggars' Guild who knows their most precious secret, unless that retirement is death.

Thieves and others on the run are blindfolded and taken all over the guild house before finally being put on the ladder and brought down into the cellar, so no thief knows exactly where the entrance is.

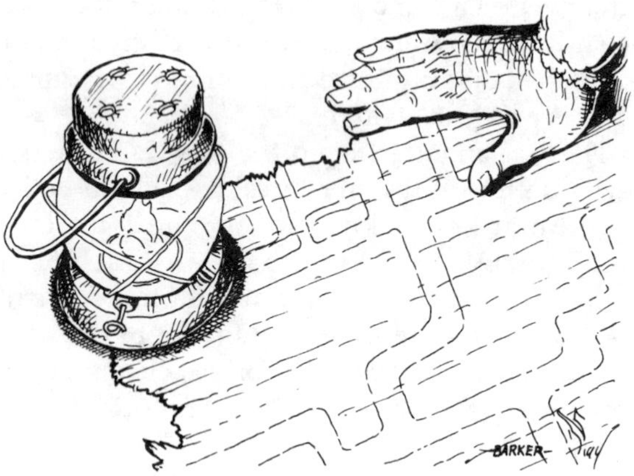

Adventure Hooks

This guild is found throughout the streets of the city and PCs can easily be dragged into Beggars' Guild plots by a guild member's simple request for alms. The two major hooks for player character adventures involve the hidden cellar and the other nonguild beggars.

- The city guards desperately want to know how to get into the secret cellar of the Beggars' guild house. They will pay a large reward—up to 200 rilks—for the information, or they may offer a party the chance to do this "service" in exchange for pardons for recent crimes, whether said crimes are real or trumped-up by the guards.

  The cellar entrance is hidden in the strongroom in the guildmaster's suite upstairs. It consists of a ladder which runs down the center of the building—inside the walls—to the cellar. To find the entrance, the PCs may need to join the Beggars' Guild long enough to be trusted with the secret.

- The real beggars of Lankhmar have had enough of the charlatans in the guild. They are organizing a takeover of the guild, by force if necessary, and they want help. This could be a job taken on either for altruistic reasons or for promise of payment when the real beggars are in control. The street beggars cannot afford to pay for hired help until they get control of the guild. A party that decides to aid the beggars should be made aware of the risk they are taking. The guild is well protected and is not easy to seize, even with a fully trained force. The underfed and ill-equipped street beggars will be more a hindrance than a help in seizing the guild house.

  Still, the rewards could be great. A small band that takes over a guild would be recognized throughout the city. The social level of each party member would rise by at least three levels. In addition, the money controlled by the Beggars' Guild is sizeable, even if the PCs only capture what's in the guildmaster's strongroom. If the party finds the treasure room, it has sacks of low value coins—a sackful is worth one gluditch.

The Charcoal Burners

Tenderloin District

One of the most secretive of guilds in the City of Sevenscore Thousand Smokes is the Charcoal Burners' Conglomerate. This secrecy stems from their responsibility for much of the smoke through their labors.

Membership of the guild is restricted to the eldest sons of current members; rare exceptions to this rule are made if a member has no sons, or no children at all, and that member is allowed to nominate a successor to the guild membership.

The members of the Charcoal Burners' Conglomerate conduct most of their business outside the city limits. Apart from charcoal, the guild is also responsible for cutting peat in the Great Marsh. Peat is often burned in winter when wood or charcoal are in short supply. It is also useful in gardens for keeping down weeds and for providing a solid foundation for seedlings.

The peat cutters work the marsh areas, and the charcoal burners work in the area south of Lankhmar. Trees are either bought from property owners or are cut down and removed by the guild when landowners want more clear space on their properties. The guild neither pays for such trees nor are they paid for cutting them down and removing them. Both sides consider it a fair exchange.

The guild has a large drying and burning kiln near the southern road leading out of the End Gate. Alone among Lankhmar's traders, the Charcoal Burners are permitted to bring their wares in through the End Gate, provided they are brought in by hand or pack and not on a wagon.

Charcoal is used for many things in Lankhmar. Its most basic use is for fuel, but it is also used by apothecaries to prepare many of their remedies. It is also used by artists for drawing, and thieves smear it on their faces when they wish to blend in with the shadows.

The guild house is always shrouded by light fog or smoke. Standing on Carter Street near the Street of the Gods, it is a five-story building of sturdy timber and stonework construction. The top two floors contain apartments used by guild members during high season, when they often put in sixteen or more hours of work per day preparing charcoal. The next floor down is occupied by the guild's offices and the senior guild members' chambers. The second floor is used mainly by the peat cutters to store their tools. The ground floor is the public face of the guild, such as it is. Open to nonmembers for only two hours each day, the walls and ceiling are covered in charcoal dust, and the floor is covered with peat moss squares which are replaced every two weeks. The atmosphere of the place is designed to turn away the curious sightseer, and it keeps all but the most hardy individuals away from the guild house. The Charcoal Burners' guild house is one of the few buildings in Lankhmar not to have any cellars.

Due to the perpetual veil of smoke around the guild house, there are rumors that the highest officers in the guild can bend the monstrous Deadly Smog to their will. While this is not true, the guild does nothing to dispel the rumors. A little thought would enable anyone to realize the rumors are false; if they had such power, the guild would have taken over the city years ago. As it is, the rumors add to the sense of mystery surrounding the guild.

Baret, the current guildmaster, is a gaunt man well over six feet tall. His height, combined with his cadaverous build, contributes to the uneasiness most people feel when meeting him. His eyes are dark brown, almost black, and what is left of his receding hair is jet black. Despite his 47 years, he has no gray in his hair or beard, nor does he show signs of slowing down to contemplate retirement. Instead, he and his advisers constantly berate the Overlord and their merchant customers about the relatively low amounts being paid for charcoal and peat moss. Due solely to his excellent bargaining and debating skills, Baret has succeeded in gaining a twenty percent increase in revenues over the last two years for only a ten percent increase in production.

Adventure Hooks

- The rumors of the guild's ability to control the Deadly Smog are gaining credence. The Overlord himself wants them proved or disproved, and the PCs are the lucky individuals who get put to the test.

  Their methods of finding the information is up to the PCs, but they must have it back to the Overlord in four days or less. The festival of Vermin Day is approaching and the Overlord wishes to rid the city of the Rat God's creatures once and for all. Sending the Deadly Smog into the sewers to clear out the rats would not involve any risk of city guards or high priced mercenaries.

  Payment for the investigation is a matter of negotiation. Payment of an outstanding fine may be appropriate, or perhaps the prestige of working for the Overlord himself is payment enough. Certainly, if the mission is successful, all surviving party members should gain one or even two social levels just by being known as the Overlord's investigators.

  Experience points are also quite variable for this job. Depending on how the task is undertaken, there may be many points for negotiating with guild members, or there may be points for using more direct methods to get to the truth. Only those members of guild officer level know the truth, and they will not reveal it unless they are in danger of being killed. Guild members will not take kindly to being roughly handled. As a consequence of this adventure, the Charcoal Burners' Conglomerate might even hire an assassin to teach the PCs a lesson.

- The Overlord is sick of Baret's complaints and wants him humbled. He doesn't want Baret's death, but he should be roughed up enough so he knows he cannot push the Overlord any more. This job should only be given to a party if they owe the Overlord a favor, or have large outstanding fines. There can be no cash payment since the Overlord has no wish to be implicated if Baret doesn't survive his "lesson."

The Company of Unusual Headgear

Plaza District

Lankhmar is home to a number of adventuring companies, some successful and others less so. Among the more flamboyant of these companies are those members of the Company of Unusual Headgear. With five, or sometimes six, members, the group's distinguishing feature is the variety of headgear owned by the adventurers.

Each commission they accept demands a new hat for each member of the group. The hats must all be identical except for size. It is remarkable that they ever complete any commissioned jobs since they rarely agree on what style their hats should be for the particular jobs. To avoid total bickering, they usually take turns to pick the hats (though those who don't choose complain loudly about the pick). The Company members have worn jester's caps, turbans, top hats, berets, or even liripipes. After each job, they never wear the hat again in public. Either they are thrown away or each member of the company has a huge box of barely worn hats stashed away somewhere.

Apart from the odd taste in hats, the company has two other quirks to distinguish it and its members from their fellows. The first is their refusal to use real names; each member is known by a nickname, and answers to nothing else. If any of them have real names, they have forgotten them since it has been so long since they were used. Their other quirk is the lack of an obvious leader. At different times, under different conditions, any one of them may take the role of company leader.

The company members rent a large room at the Rising Moon, on the top floor. They spend much time in and around their home because few people take them seriously. This is a mistake, for they are a capable band and often successful because they are so easy to underestimate. The Company of Unusual Headgear makes an excellent rival or ally group for characters adventuring in Nehwon. NPC secondary weapons, skills, and abilities are left to the DM's discretion.

Coalface
T5/F5; SL 2; AL CG; AC 10; MV 12; hp 32; THAC0 16; #AT 1; Dmg 1d6 (short sword); Str 15; Dex 14; Con 13; Int 17; Wis 10; Cha 14; age 24

Coalface is a little under six feet tall and is slightly built. He is the imagination of the company, and he is the one who comes up with the most outrageous hat designs, and plans of what to do when work is scarce. His plans and ideas are always orthodox, unlike Neurth's. It is Coalface who keeps the company inspired to go on to bigger and more ambitious commissions time after time. Eventually, it will also be Coalface who gets them all killed with his nonchalant approach to danger.

Like Neurth, Coalface is fascinated by women. Unlike Neurth, he often allows this fascination to cloud his judgement of reality. He does not know how to resist an attractive woman or refuse her anything. This has caused some ripples in the company by Coalface accepting jobs for the company that paid poorly just because the client was a woman. Coalface is no longer allowed to accept commissions unless at least one other company member is present and agrees to the terms.

Coalface has a slightly distorted view on time. If a job needs to be done in ten days, then the planning should be started in the evening in nine days time. Or is it the evening in ten days time? Coalface is never quite sure. If not for Toady's steadying influence, Coalface might have been murdered by an irate client years ago. The rest of the company regard Coalface as both a guru at planning and a complete failure at timing. He doesn't understand why.

Coalface is the most likely of the company to leave and settle down to a mundane lifestyle. He isn't likely to do so until he meets the right woman, but he thinks that's every one he meets. Toady has saved him from himself so far.

The Dunce
T8; SL 3; AL N; AC 7 (due to *ring of protection +3*); MV 12; hp 22; THAC0 17; #AT 1; Dmg 2d4 + 1 (broad sword and Strength bonus); Str 16; Dex 12; Con 12; Int 7; Wis 9; Cha 13; age 30

The Dunce is aptly named due to his low intelligence and his slow wit. He can read, but his writing is nearly impossible to decipher. He looks appropriately dressed in a tall conical cap with a large red D on it, which he wears when not on a job. His comrades have told him the D is for "Don't fight with me" and he believes them.

The Dunce is dark haired, and well over six feet tall. His height is an advantage when the group finds it necessary to break into a building. The Company of Unusual Headgear (and the Thieves' Guild and Midnight and scores of others) learned long ago that few people bar windows above street level and group members often use the Dunce's shoulders to reach the second floor.

The Dunce can be relied upon to do only one thing—be unreliable. If he is needed on a job at midday, he is told to be there at ten in the morning. That way, he might arrive by one in the afternoon. He has a laid back attitude to life that drives the others to despair. The Dunce is never nervous or tense, but he certainly makes others feel that way with his lackadaisical attitude.

As the oldest member of the company, the Dunce should be taking a share of the responsibility for getting and completing contracts. Unfortunately, acting in a responsible manner is not in his makeup. There are always other things on his mind and he often easily forgets where he's going or why he's doing something. Toady or one of the others often has to go and look for him to make sure he comes to a job.

He is a founding member of the Company, his membership granted for life if he wants it. Despite the problems with the Dunce, his height and strong arm are useful in a tight situation. It hasn't yet occurred to the others to encourage the Dunce to leave by his choice, should they really wish to be rid of him and his limited faculties.

Neurth
T2/WW2; SL 0; AL CG; AC 7 (due to Dexterity); MV 12; hp 10; THAC0 20; #AT 1; Dmg 1d4 (dagger); Str 13; Dex 17; Con 14; Int 13; Wis 9; Cha 14; age 23

Neurth is the newest member of the Company, and is an oddity even among this band. Neurth has dark curly hair and stands a little under six feet. His build is very slim, as his body is nearly straight up and down between the shoulders and hips. The others frequently wonder aloud at what holds his pants up. Certainly, it is neither his belt (which is always loose) nor his suspenders (since he doesn't wear any).

The company allowed Neurth to join their ranks because he claimed to have money—they were almost destitute at the time—and partly because they felt sorry for him. It turned out that Neurth's money was enough for one decent meal for them all, but they learned of his persuasive talents. The group was so impressed with his ability to con others that he was immediately invited to stay. Neurth's boyish looks and innocent facial expressions make him so easy to trust; one day soon, his looks will get him into trouble with a woman unless the rest of the company keep him away from them.

Neurth's special gift is his ability to lighten a tense moment with a funny, often ribald story. His fascination with women features prominently in most of his stories. While engaging and fun to be around, Neurth's most annoying trait is his habit of answering a question he was asked several hours ago when he is being asked something entirely different now. After a few episodes of this, most people sift through their memories when Neurth speaks, trying to put his answer in context and never trying to fit it into the current topic.

Sassy

BW4/T4; SL 2; AL CN; AC 7 (due to *ring of protection +3*); MV 12; hp 22; THAC0 17; #AT 1; Dmg 1d4 (dagger); Str 12; Dex 13; Con 12; Int 15; Wis 12; Cha 10; age 30

Sassy is the shortest member of the company, at 5½ feet tall. He always refers to his height that way, believing it sounds more impressive than "5 feet, 6 inches." Nobody else seems to know the difference.

He is solidly built, but has more fat and less muscle than is good for an adventurer. He is also not very attractive. This may in part be due to his delvings into black magic, though many Lankhmarts will attest he was unattractive long before he started fooling with magic.

Sassy has curly black hair that always looks like it needs brushing, and he has mismatched eyes—one blue and one brown. His eyes are sunk into his skull, making him look almost like a cadaver despite his stockiness; he can be quite frightening the first time anyone looks at him.

Although he is a little shy, his manner is quite friendly. Those who get to know him find that he can be a lot of fun at social occasions. His normally reserved nature cannot resist playing jokes on people of high station, and he never seems to catch the blame because the nobles believe his shy act.

The other members of the company are a little concerned at Sassy's delvings into magic and worry that, if he continues to explore further in that direction, he may become a danger to himself and to them. If that happens, Sassy will be asked to leave the company. Sassy himself knows of their fears and has not yet decided whether to stay in the group with the only friends he has, or to embrace the path of the black wizard and forsake everything else.

As a shy practical joker, Sassy seldom uses obvious or flamboyant spells, preferring to use more subtle magic to accomplish his ends. Even when pulling a prank, he prefers subtlety over crudity, partly to hide the source of the magic.

Toady

BW3/T5; SL 2; AL CG; AC 6 (due to Dexterity); MV 12; hp 21; THAC0 18; #AT 1; Dmg 1d4 (dagger); Str 14; Dex 18; Con 15; Int 17; Wis 12; Cha 10; age 26

Toady is a tall man of solid build, physically fit but not burly or muscle bound. He fancies himself a ladies' man but he hasn't the courage to approach a lady. In addition, his clothing puts off many potential paramours, since Toady's odd dress sense is not limited to his hats—many of his clothes clash with each other (and anyone else's!) but he doesn't seem to care or even notice.

He is slow to anger, an admirable trait since the others make jokes at his expense quite often. There isn't an evil bone in Toady's body, which is why he switched from the path of black magic before it corrupted him. He is reluctant to use what magic he knows unless he has no choice, preferring to rely on his strength to keep him alive.

Toady is the most reliable member of the company, and is often the only one who remembers what job they took on the night before. The other members of the company often remark that Toady is like a mother hen, as he constantly reminds them of their obligations to complete contracts.

Toady has a preference for gadgetry and decoration over standard equipment. Where most folk would wear knee boots for comfort and protection, Toady has his boots painted with scenes of past jobs. He also has a habit of attaching small decorative wings to the ankles of any footwear he owns.

Adventure Hooks

Given the outward quirks of this company, it is relatively simple to come up with adventure hooks to work them into a scenario, for good or ill.

- Honarth, an honest hatmaker located in the Plaza District, is found murdered in the alleyway just outside his shop's back door. His purse, the strongbox from behind his counter, and a number of hats are missing from the shop. Coalface and Sassy were seen at Honarth's shop an hour before the murder was discovered, arguing loudly with each other and with Honarth. If the city guards search their rooms at the Rising Moon, they find Honarth's strongbox. The Company did not murder the hatmaker; they simply ran afoul of the Thieves' Guild on their previous job, and, in retaliation, the thieves have framed the group for murder.
- Brawls are an infrequent occurrence at the Rising Moon, especially among its regular crowd. However, newcomers in town always mix it up with the natives when they don't know any better. A number of Mingol mercenaries have decided to pick a fight with the Company members, who are all enjoying a drink after a successful mission. The Mingols don't like their newest hats, which are wire and leather imitations of Mingol war helms. The PCs can be drawn into the resulting brawl as allies or enemies (or they, rather than the Mingols, could be the instigators of the fight).
- The PCs have been hired by a rich merchant and his wife to safeguard their daughters while they travel outside the city for a week. Unfortunately, the young women caught the attentions of Coalface and Neurth when the Company acted as guards at the merchant's last gala, and they are infatuated with them. One of the girls, Khalia, also seeks a life of adventure and wants to run away and become a ranger. The PCs must protect them from Neurth and Coalface, and keep Khalia from running away.

The Embalmers' Guild

Plaza District

Located immediately, and conveniently, behind the Fellowship of Physician's Hall, the Embalmers' guild house is a place most Lankhmarts prefer to attend only once, after they are dead. It has four floors above ground and at least two below ground.

The underground areas are kept cool by the insular effect of the ground and the airflow over large blocks of ice. It is here that the deceased are prepared for their final journey. Corpses are embalmed and kept for five days before burial or cremation, to ensure that the spirit has departed before the funeral. There is room for up to 100 bodies in the cellars, but there are rarely more than 20 at any time. Embalming fluids and other substances, such as facial makeup, rouge, and mascara (used to make the corpses presentable for funerals), are stored in the lowest level of the guild house.

The ground floor is the public face of the guild. There, the duty embalmer greets the bereaved and arranges to collect the corpse (if it hasn't been delivered already), and discusses funeral arrangements. All funeral details are passed on to the Gravediggers' Guild each evening, along with payment for that day's funerals. All financial matters for funerals are handled through this guild.

Prices for funerals vary depending on how much the bereaved can afford. The average funeral costs 30 rilks, payable in advance. Nobles and the wealthy may have a casket costing 50 rilks or more, with fittings of gold or silver. These funerals cost three times as much as the casket, also payable in advance. Paupers are buried at the city's expense, but paupers' bodies are not embalmed and are buried within two days in mass graves.

The next two floors are administrative areas, used for record keeping. It is here that a genealogist may find details of ancestors, provided one knows where to look. There is a two agol fee for researching each name. Nonguild members are not allowed on these floors without a guild member in attendance. The records are not complete or fully accurate, but if a person's name appears, they are definitely dead and buried.

The top floor is the home of the guildmaster. Currently, Lygin is the guildmaster and he looks more akin to one of his customers than a living human. He is gaunt with a pasty complexion and he always wears drab gray or dingy white clothes. His sunken eyes are sullen and dark, and his hands are cold to the touch, not that many people touch his hands. No one other than a guild member with an appointment is allowed into Lygin's home. He has no guards, but there are rumors that he is related to a highly ranked member of the Slayers' Brotherhood, so he is rarely bothered by intruders.

Adventure Hooks

Current rumors about the Embalmers' Guild involve the recent delivery of ornate coffin fittings. The silver fittings are worth five gluditches, but rumors place their worth much higher. Lygin is worried about the fittings and wants them guarded against the Thieves' Guild, or Midnight's band. The party will be paid 3 agols per guard per day and they must provide a 24-hour guard with at least two guards day and night. The guild will supply meals to the guards on duty.

Midnight has no interest in the fittings, but the Thieves' Guild has access to a smelter and is very interested in the silver fittings. The fittings equal 200 rilks of raw silver.

Thieves will infiltrate the guild house on the second night the characters are on guard. They will drug the PCs' food—PCs must save against poison or fall asleep for 1–4 hours. There are twice as many thieves as PCs, and each thief is armed with a dagger (THAC0 19, AC 8 due to Dexterity, 15 hp each). They will fight only if cornered, and seek escape once they get the silver. All the thieves are masked and dressed in black. There is no chance of identifying them later.

For each thief killed, the party gains 120 XP, or 90 XP for forcing a thief to flee. In addition, if the heist is successfully thwarted, each player character gains one social level. They also draw the attention of the Thieves' Guild, who might try to have them killed, or frame them for some other crime.

The Taverners' Guild

Tenderloin District

All port cities have a larger number of "watering holes" than their landlocked counterparts. In comparison, Lankhmar has more taverns than most port cities, and they are not confined to the docks, though that area is where they are the most plentiful.

When all the taverns in a city are guild-affiliated, and there are many taverns, it follows that the Taverners' Guild is a powerful force in local politics and the city's economy.

Located where the Mercantile, Cash, and Tenderloin Districts join, the Taverners' guild house is not very impressive from the outside. It is a seven-story building, one of the tallest in Lankhmar, but it lacks windows, balconies, or any external features at all above the first floor. It looks like an enormous barn stuck on top of two floors of living space, and that is almost exactly what it is.

The ground floor contains all the administration and clerical office space. There are four clerks employed here full time, around the clock. During big celebrations, up to four more staff persons are brought in, usually on a roster system, from the taverns. All tavern orders for liquor come through the offices, and all the guild's orders for supplies come out of here. Even a taverner who has his own brewery or distillery and is supplying himself moves his product through the guild house, at least on paper. For convenience, the stock isn't actually moved; the taverner just pays a fee as if he had bought the liquor from the guild.

The first floor also has some living quarters and these are used mainly by the guards. Guards are supplied by the taverners in the city to the guild house on a roster basis. Small taverns supply one guard for a day once a month. The bigger the tavern, the more the taverner is expected to help with security at the guild house. Most taverners send a bouncer or two when it is their turn. A few will send a family member, but only if the roster requires them for no more than a day. At any time, there are ten to twelve guards in the guild house, and they are provided with a wide assortment of weapons for the guild's defense.

The upper floors contain the reason the guild is so protective of the guild house. There is really only one additional floor—the second. It is stacked high with alcohol, from the most common beer to the rarest vintage wine from the vineyards of the Eastern Lands. The value of the stock in normal times is several thousand gluditches, but the possibility of more than a few hundred rilks worth being stolen is quite remote.

The biggest danger to the stock is fire and the guild has taken extraordinary steps to protect the building and its contents. Alone among the buildings and people of Lankhmar, the guards and staff of the guild house conduct fire drills at least every two days. It may be boring and repetitious, but the alternative is far worse. Should fire destroy the building, or even a significant portion of it, the taverners whose people were on roster will be punished severely. The guards will be put to death if the fire doesn't kill them. The "responsible" taverner and his family will be indentured to the guild for five years, keeping only enough to survive while they pay back the guild for its losses. At the end of the five years, the tavern becomes the property of the guild and is sold at auction. Not surprisingly, taverners and their staff take guard duty very seriously.

The floor of the warehouse has been reinforced to hold the weight of the rows of shelving stacked to the false ceiling some fifty feet above. The false ceiling is a barrier against the summer heat, which can spoil the liquor.

Ladders are built onto the shelving at intervals, and huge oak beams run the length of each passageway. The beams are grooved and have been worked to permit block and tackle to be quickly slung anywhere in the warehouse.

Large barrels and kegs are stored on the floor or on the first two rows of shelves, which were made high enough to hold 18 gallon kegs. These contain mostly ale and beer, or an occasional cheap variety of wine.

Smaller kegs and barrels are stored next, on rows of shelves designed to take up to nine gallon kegs. Most kegs this size contain fine ale or even mead, and fortified wines. These kegs can also hold strong spirits.

The rest of the shelves are stacked with vessels of all shapes and sizes, and made of virtually any nonporous material available. They contain rare drinks and liquors from all the cities and lands across Nehwon. If a traveler in any tavern requests a drink from his home town, the barkeep can get it within a few minutes at any time of the day or night. It is the boast of the Taverners' Guild that they stock at least one of every alcoholic beverage available anywhere in Nehwon. So far, they have been correct.

With such an investment, the guild does not take kindly to folk running their own small breweries or stills. Home-brewing for personal consumption is tolerated, since the guild controls much of the supply of home-brewing materials. Importing liquor privately is discouraged, usually by a couple of brawny men breaking things in the house of the importer. Even the Overlord fears to bring in more than an occasional flagon of exotic wine.

The guild maintains a careful watch on the Plaza of Dark Delights at night, ensuring that all beverages sold were handled through the guild. While the guild does not care what is sold, or who buys it, they do care about their percentage of the profits and come down hard on guild breakers. Few vendors transgress twice and any who are caught twice are usually drowned in whatever they were selling, as a warning to others.

Adventure Hooks

The Taverners' Guild pays well for information about bootleggers. There is a standing reward of 150 rilks for any information which is found to be true.

So, many people down on their luck keep a sharp lookout for furtive alcohol vendors. Out of work adventurers are the most common informants, since they often go from vendor to vendor, drinking their last earnings while they wait for their next job.

Countess Kronia arranged for a small keg of rare Kognab wine to be sent to her estate. Unfortunately, she did not make the arrangements with the Taverners' Guild. The keg arrived in Lankhmar and disappeared. The courier was found face down in the Hlal. He was covered in cuts and bruises and obviously perished fighting. Kronia wants her wine, and has offered 300 rilks to anyone who recovers it. Most Lankhmarts believe the keg is in the Taverners' guild house and, in that case, it can stay there. Not only would they have to get past the staff and the guards, they would have to find the keg in the warehouse. This could take six or seven hours if you didn't know where to look.

The keg is worth two gluditches, and on the remote chance that someone will try to steal it, the guild has hidden it in the cellar of the Rising Moon, behind a number of 18 gallon kegs of ale.

The guild plans to return it to Kronia, eventually, for its full value. Since she has already paid for it once, it will be an expensive lesson to her and all the nobility about the perils of crossing the Taverners. The Countess will pay the reward, or even a little more, to anyone who helps her. She will be especially eager when she hears from the Taverners, since paying for something twice is not Kronia's idea of good business. Once the guild has made its demands, Kronia will increase the reward money to 400 rilks.

Experience for this adventure depends mostly on whether the keg is retrieved by stealth or by combat.

The Vermin Catchers

Plaza District

In the Plaza District, on Festival Street near the corner of Beggars' Boulevard, is the guild house of the Vermin Catchers' Guild. It is really four separate buildings, all joined by passageways invisible from outside the houses.

The main building, and the only one generally known to belong to the guild, is five stories high and has no underground levels. From the outside, the guild house is more like a miniature fortress, with two armed guards standing to either side of the entrance. Other guards thoroughly check everyone who enters who is not a known guild member for concealed weapons. The guards are present even at night when the guild house is closed for business. After dark, the guards number at least eight. To keep themselves alert, they work only two-hour shifts.

The ground floor is the administration area, where those who need the services of the "rat catchers" file their requests for assistance. It is staffed by at least three clerks at all times during the day. Each of them has a sword or loaded crossbow within easy reach behind the counter.

The upper floors are the storage areas for cages, traps, and poisons used in the eradication of vermin. There is a considerable quantity of arsenic and even some cyanide in the poisons storage locker on the top floor. During the day, there are always at least four guild members on each floor engaged in testing and maintaining the equipment. Each guildsman is armed with a sword, and they are generally left on the floor, out of their scabbards. As it considered bad luck to draw a sword without drawing blood, each man makes a cut on his arm at the end of his shift before returning his sword to its scabbard.

The leftmost building is three stories high and it also has no rooms underground. From the front, it seems to be a normal dwelling, and the apartments are rented out to anyone who wants to pay for them. But it is a facade. Behind the outer row of apartments are the rooms of most of the unmarried guildsmen. Their rooms can only be reached through a hidden passage from the main guild house. Each man has a small arsenal in his room, always ready and in easy reach.

The rightmost building also has a facade of apartments that anyone other than a known worshipper of the Rat God can rent. There are more guild quarters behind the facade of this four-story building, and two basement levels which provide easy access to the sewers. This fact is unknown to those in Lankhmar Below. The ground floor and first basement level are marshalling areas for guildsmen about to enter the undercity. The second floor holds the guild's main arsenal, which includes short swords, crossbows, flasks of greek fire, and many vials of poison. Many swords and crossbow bolts are tipped or coated with poisons or silver for use against the rats and wererats.

The guildmaster's residence is in the rear building. Outwardly, the building is a modest dwelling, a simple house of only one floor, and there is no reason to believe it is anything else. There is nothing to connect the residents of the house to the Vermin Catchers and city records do not show the guild as the owner of the building. The secret doorway to the main guild house is well hidden, and the guildmaster is careful to only use it when no one other than his family is present. The identity of the guildmaster is always kept a close secret, since there is a permanent price on his head, whoever he is. A number of other guildsmen live in tenements across the road from the guildmaster, and there are always a few of them on watch in case the rat folk decide to attack. These men remain unobtrusive at all times as they do not wish to give away the secret of the house.

The reason for all the security and secrecy is that the Vermin Catchers are virtually at war with the worshippers of the Rat God, and are certainly at war with Lankhmar Below. There seems to be a disagreement over what exactly constitutes vermin. The guild says rats are vermin, and the Rat God's followers say that humans are vermin. Since they cannot agree, and each wants to exterminate the other, battles are quite common. The rats and their human followers seldom attack in daylight, preferring the cover of darkness to aid them against a well-prepared foe. They cannot attack from below since the main guild house has no cellar, and they do not know the other buildings are attached from the inside. The rats believe all the defenders are housed in the guild house.

On the other hand, the guild prefers to raid the sewers and tunnels in the daytime, when the inhabitants are mostly asleep and a little slow to respond. Ambient light from above is also greatest in the middle of the day. The only artificial light used in the sewers comes from bullseye lanterns which are lit on the surface and kept hooded while the men are in the tunnels.

As the rats of Lankhmar Below are quite intelligent, they are aware of the guild's strategy and always post guards in the tunnels where they expect attacks to come from. Thus, the guild rarely succeed in surprising any significant groups of rats.

Even though they carry greek fire, the guild members seldom use it. The air in the sewers has a high level of methane gas in it, and any spark or open flame could cause a massive fiery explosion in the sewers and tunnels beneath the city. While this would do severe damage to the rats, it would most likely kill the human who started it and any others in the nearby sewer network. Many other humans would be injured or even killed by the blast as the fire swept up and out of manhole covers throughout the city. The only time a guildsman might use the fire is if he is being overwhelmed by those who dwell below and he wants to take his attackers down with him. Numbers are the only real advantage the rats and their friends have, but it is a significant one.

Adventure Hooks

The eternal war between the rats and the Vermin Catchers is one which no party of adventurers can hope to win, or even to influence in any large way. It is also a war in which the careful and clever party can make a name for themselves as well as a sizeable amount of money.

The Vermin Catchers are always on the lookout for adventurers brave (silly) enough to venture below and wipe out a nest or two of rats. The pay is quite good, as much as one rilk per mission for proof of wiping out at least one nest. In general, freelancers will be paid one agol per dead rat. Of course, it is not widely advertised that the guild hires freelancers to do its dirty work. That would defeat the purpose of having a guild. But, the guildsmen believe it is worth quietly paying a bounty on dead rats rather than risk their own necks in constant assaults on the sewers.

Payment for killing wererats is one rilk per corpse. For a successful raid on the Rat God's temple, the party can keep half the loot they find. The other half is to cover the guild's likely costs in accepting responsibility for the raid. Success against the rat folk will raise a person's social level in the Vermin Catchers' guild as well as with anyone who deals with the guild. It will also be likely to draw the attention of the rats' friends in Lankhmar above to the party, and the PCs may find their lives far more interesting and busy than before.

A successful raid against the temple is unlikely to bring any prestige outside the guild, since the PCs cannot take responsibility for the raid. To do so would bring the wrath of the temple on their heads as well as the authorities. While they do not like the Rat God, attacking a well established temple is not something that is encouraged in Lankhmar. For fear of annoying the Gods, it is an offense to attack any religious building east of Pimp Street.

Minor Guilds in the Plaza and Tenderloin Districts

Life in Lankhmar revolves around the various guilds. Many of them will never feature in the lives of your characters, but one never knows how the intrigues of the City of Sevenscore Thousand Smokes will manifest themselves. Here is a brief outline of those guilds that are not listed in this book or in the *City of Adventure* source book.

The Barbers' Guild

While one of the smaller guilds of the city, the Barbers' Guild of Lankhmar is quite a lucrative conglomerate. None of the barbers within the city limits are not guild-affiliated. Through their guild connections, barbers can buy high-quality razors and knives more cheaply than other individuals in the city.

In addition to being barbers, many members are associated with other guilds like the Physicians' Fellowship and the Slayers' Brotherhood. These barbers can respectively provide some basic medical help (such as bleeding, leeches, or basic stitches) or they can set up assassinations (a simple slipped razor during a shave) for the Slayers. The latter is a rare association, and the Barbers' Guild is held to be a generally honest and beneficial fellowship.

The Chandlers' Guild

The Chandlers comprise one of the richest guilds in Lankhmar as the providers of a major necessity. The guild members work in the Craft Street warehouses in the northern Tenderloin District, making candles and distilling lamp oil for use throughout the city. As everyone needs candles and oil, their products net an astounding amount of coin each month when they sell their wares to the public. They, in turn, pay goodly amounts to the Thieves' Guild for protection from theft or extortion.

The Taverners' Guild and a few other business guilds buy special bulk orders to distribute to their guild members at a better rate than normally available. The temples and the Overlord have special candles and oils created for their uses, like special perfumes or herbs infused within the candle wax. There are even rumors about the city that the Slayers' Brotherhood pays to have poisons put into candles, and the burning candle creates a poison gas, but no one knows if such a candle has ever been made.

The Gravediggers' Guild

The Gravediggers' guild house is located quite near that of the Embalmers' Guild. This arrangement is quite convenient for both guilds to operate their closely-tied professions. There is no cemetery in Lankhmar, although some noble houses have family crypts in their grounds or beneath their homes. There are two cemeteries outside the city. The first is reached through the End Gate, and it is where most of Lankhmar's dead are buried. The second cemetery is much smaller and is reached through the Grand Gate. It is reserved for nobles who do not have family crypts. As a public service, the Gravediggers "bury" even paupers who cannot afford a funeral. These folk are taken to the Great Marsh in a pauper's coffin, a coffin with a hinged flap on one end. Once in the Marsh, the coffin is upended and the shrouded corpse is dumped into a convenient mass grave.

The Laborers' Guild

On the border of the Plaza and Tenderloin Districts is the Laborers' guild house. Technically located in the Tenderloin District, the members insist it is in the Plaza District, since that locale is at least one social level higher than the rough-and-tumble Tenderloin District. The Laborers are often in demarcation disputes with the Carters' and Toters' Guild over their guild responsibilities, and small scuffles are regular occurrences. They never amount to anything, as both guilds would rather get the job done than fight over who should do it. Eventually, the two guilds will probably merge and solve the problem permanently.

The Salters' Guild

The Salters' guild house is located in the Tenderloin District near the Marsh Gate. The members of this guild make their living by preserving meat and other foodstuffs for those who can afford it. Their raw salt comes mainly from the Great Marsh, and their customers are mostly from the Noble District. Every so often, the guild has trouble because someone gets food poisoning and they always blame it on bad meat. The guild members take their work very seriously and any member who lets the guild standards slip is expelled and may even face murder charges if someone dies from eating bad meat.

The Shinglers' and Roofers' Guild

The Shinglers and Roofers are located in a four-story building in the Plaza District, near the Plaza itself. Having a high level view of the entire city in the course of their duties, many members of this guild act as scouts or spies for a second employer while they are carrying out their public function of fixing roofs. As long as the roofing job is done correctly and quickly, the guildmaster turns a blind eye to this extra-curricular work. Of late, however, a number of guild members have been arrested for thieving and other offenses. The members admit to watching the places that were robbed from their roof repair jobs, but they claim they were framed by the Thieves' Guild.

The Soap Makers' Guild

The Soap Makers' Guild maintains a decrepit two-story wooden guild house in the Tenderloin District near the Marsh Gate. The Overlord has banned the making of soap inside the city, as the stench is often overwhelming. So, all the rendering is done out in the Great Marsh. The guild often hires mercenaries as guards since the inhabitants of the marsh are not always friendly towards the smelly soap makers. Perfuming is also done in the marsh, as the rendered soap must be molded and perfumed within a few minutes or the scent evaporates and is useless.

The Tanners' Guild

The Tanners' guild house is just off the Plaza of Dark Delights. It acts as a clearing house for hides of wild animals. Members are free to buy domestic hides wherever they like. With the interests of its members uppermost, the guild's buyers drive a hard bargain for all hides, selling them on to members at only a little over cost price. Hides of rare or dangerous animals fetch top prices, and traders have been known to sell a hide to the guild, then try to steal it back.

Guild Feuds & Rivalries

There are always internal disagreements and problems within the guilds themselves, as members jockey for positions of greater influence among their fellows. The combination of money and politics rarely allows for easy cooperation among guild members, but alliances and compromises are made to allow the guild to conduct its business for the general (if not specific) gain of its overall membership. Once the guild is organized, its activities are as well.

Serious problems result if one guild's activities infringe on another guild's assumed responsibilities and territories. Guilds often pit themselves against each other until one guild is the clear victor; these rivalries can often take years to settle, during which fighting between rival guild members causes much strife and death on both sides. Open warfare rarely happens between the guilds, not due to any cool-headedness on the guilds' parts, but due to edicts by the Overlord to at least partially maintain the status quo and peace of the city.

Currently, members of the Laborers' Guild and the Carters' and Toters' Guild are clashing in the back alleys, their guilds locked in dispute over which guild has control over the hauling of products for the markets. Neither guild wishes to give up their shares of the shipping and hauling rights (and the fees that go with them), though both guilds want the fighting to end so they can do their jobs that much easier.

CHAPTER 2

NPCs of Lankhmar

Angrew the Blacksmith

Plaza District

Located along the outer wall of Lankhmar are several stables and smithies. Among them is Angrew the blacksmith.

Angrew is on the small side for a blacksmith, being only about 170 pounds and standing five feet eight inches tall. He is broad shouldered and his frame is well muscled. No fat shows on his often naked upper body.

He is a friendly person, and his blue eyes twinkle when he smiles, which is often. Angrew is a man who really loves his work and doesn't mind showing it.

His smithy is neat and tidy, and everything is always where it should be. The forge is not large, but is very efficient, and Angrew can make anything from a simple horseshoe to a two-handed sword with the tools and materials he has at hand.

Angrew's wares are always of the utmost quality, yet he charges no more than other smiths do for their lesser goods. He is one of the old-fashioned breed of workers who believe that things should be done right or not at all. Other members of the Blacksmiths' Guild do not always agree with him, but he is a dangerous man to cross. On the rare occasions when he is attacked in the smithy, he wields his mallet like a mighty warhammer, and has smashed more than one skull in his time. Many people believe he is one of the strongest men in Lankhmar, comparable to the mighty Fafhrd himself.

Angrew puts his success down to his worship of Kos, and his rigid following of Kos' doctrine that everything should be done to perfection. Although he has no conscious knowledge of magic, Angrew's constant chants to Kos while he hammers away at his anvil have enabled him to imbue nearly everything he makes with a little devout magic. Horse shod in Angrew's smithy rarely lose their footing, even in the roughest terrain. Chains forged by Angrew are almost impossible to break. His crossbow points and arrow heads are second to none in sharpness, giving them a nonmagical +1 on damage. However, they don't allow them to hit creatures requiring magic weapons to be hit.

Though all of his work is outstanding, it is for his swords that Angrew is most famous. Even Rivis Rightby knows the work of Angrew is at least as good as his own, though he would never admit it. Whether it be a short sword or a seven foot long two handed blade, Angrew's weapons have a keen edge and absolutely perfect balance. Each of them gains a bonus of +1 for attack and damage rolls, and, by the blessing of Kos, they can hit creatures hit only by magical weapons.

Strangely, because the magic in the swords is divinely granted rather than the usual enchantment from a black wizard, Angrew's weapons do not respond to any form of magical detection, nor do they shed light or do other things one might expect from magical blades. Also due to the nature of their magic, Angrew's weapons are immune to the effects of *dispel magic* and *anti-magic shell*. A blade's magic can be cancelled only if the wielder knowingly commits a chaotic act while wielding the sword.

Effectively, in the hands of anyone not of lawful alignment, the sword quickly becomes mundane in every way, although still of finest quality workmanship. Due to these often short-lived enchantments no one, not even Angrew himself, realizes that his works are enchanted.

Angrew lives above the stable behind his smithy, with his wife and three children. His elder son is nearly ten and will soon start his training as his father's apprentice. Like most trades in Lankhmar, blacksmithing tends to be a family affair. His second child, a daughter, is learning to dance and do acrobatics. She will either become an entertainer or perhaps a cat-burglar. Angrew's younger son, and his favorite of the three children, is only five, but has already decided to become a priest but he has not chosen a deity yet. Angrew is not keen on this idea as he cannot conceive of a family member worshipping anyone but Kos, and Kos is not lenient with priests who fail him.

Adventure Hooks

It has finally come to the attention of the Mercenaries' Guild that Angrew can apparently make magical weapons. What they don't understand is why only some of his weapons are magical, yet all cost the same. The guild wants to know Angrew's intentions. Is he selling magical weapons to those people he likes, and nonmagical ones to those he doesn't?

Angrew, naturally, has no idea what the guild is talking about. If he were to make magical weapons, he admits freely that he would charge far more for them than he does. In addition, he would almost certainly be forced to sell them exclusively to the Overlord and his forces.

This logic will finally get through to the mercenaries, but they still wish to know just what is going on. The equally mystified and curious Angrew wants to know too, once he's aware of his "magic touch." He doesn't like being bullied, and he likes being accused of cheating his customers even less.

So, the PCs can be hired or sent by the Mercenaries' Guild to find out the circumstances surrounding Angrew's work. Alternatively, they may be friends or regular customers of Angrew, and helping a friend in need draws the PCs into trouble with the mercenaries.

Either way, they are going to be hard pressed to find the answer. Angrew's weapons are not aligned toward good or evil, but they are aligned toward law and chaos. So, a lawful evil person can wield one of Angrew's swords as a +1 weapon, just as a lawful good one can. A white wizard could cast a *know alignment* spell to learn about the blades or their owners, but to do so would risk an accusation of spying.

If the truth is uncovered, Angrew will not want the information made public. It would invite the wrath of the black wizards who believe they have exclusive rights when it comes to making magic items of any nature. It would also have every idiot about to embark on their first monster hunt pestering him for one of his special swords. If he can't explain that to the Mercenaries' agents, he may just have to kill them to keep his secret.

The Black Knight

Plaza District

For the last few days, a stranger has been roaming the streets of Lankhmar, concentrating around the Marsh Gate during daylight hours and the Plaza of Dark Delights in the early evening. He is dressed in black metal plate armor from head to toe and he comes into the city on a black charger each morning.

An armored knight is a rare enough sight on Nehwon, so most are known throughout the lands. But this one is different, as no one has heard of him and he has refused all requests to identify himself, beyond his title as the Black Knight.

His behavior is a little strange for a knight. He has issued an open challenge of nonlethal combat to anyone who will stand against him. Challengers must wager at least three rilks on the battle, and he will wager at least double what the challenger puts down. The winner retains all the money wagered and, after two days, the knight had amassed 180 rilks by conservative estimates.

His antics have annoyed many folk in Lankhmar. The Society of Joyous and Sorrowful Comedians, Rapturous Playactors, Graceful Dancers, and Melodious Songsters (known colloquially as the Entertainers' Society) claim the knight is providing entertainment and he should be made to join their ranks (so the guild can get its cut of the knight's winnings). Members of the Slayers' Brotherhood have threatened his life if he continues to fight in public. Several residents are insisting the Black Knight pay for damage to their houses caused when he threw opponents through windows or doors.

Everyone wants to know who he is and where he comes from. His claim to be an Ilthmart is patently untrue, but no one is brave or foolish enough to dispute him to his face. Attempts to follow him to his lodgings have proved fruitless. All that has been discovered is that he leaves the city each night, well after dark, and seemingly disappears into the blackness of the Nehwon night. By first light each morning, he is back in the city, taking on all comers in a flagrant taunt at both guilds who want him stopped.

As he has not broken any laws, the city guards are both unable and unwilling to interfere. Besides, if the Slayers are busy with the knight, they are not causing any grief to regular Lankhmarts.

As far as anyone can tell, the Black Knight is about five feet six inches tall and seems of slim build underneath his armor. He fights right handed, but he can fight left handed and has done so on a couple of occasions. He carries a bastard sword and shield, although he does not use them in his bouts since the challenge was for nonlethal combat. The device on his shield is a sleek, rampant black reptile with wings; it is a black dragon, but there are no dragons in Nehwon, and few truly recognize this device as such.

Although his horse has some barding, it is always tethered or stabled very near where the knight is meeting the day's challengers. Because the combats are nonlethal, the knight's warhorse would only make the odd situation more difficult. Many are wondering why the knight bothers to have the horse, let alone bard it (an expensive prospect on any world), if it is little more than an observer. The answer is quite simple. The knight expects the Slayers to come after him soon, either for their own benefit or at the request of the Entertainers' Society. The Slayers are simply waiting for the entertainers to request action, so they can be paid for doing the job. If the request does not come in the next few days, it is likely the Slayers will act on their own behalf.

The final mystery with this knight is that he travels alone. All the known knights have at least a squire, and many have a sizeable retinue trailing in their wake. The Black Knight travels alone and apparently tends his horse and his weapons himself. There is some speculation among his younger challengers that he is looking for a squire and has chosen this unusual method to find a suitable one. If this is true, he has not yet succeeded, since every challenger has left the battle bruised in both ego and body, and lightened in the pocket.

Adventure Hooks

The Entertainers' Society wants to know who the knight is and they want him either to stop his antics or to pay for guild membership. The PCs can be guild members sent to investigate and possibly challenge the knight. They could alternatively be members of the Slayers' Brotherhood hired or sent by their guildmaster to either investigate or kill the knight. They may also be freelancers hired by the entertainers, an option that will bring the unwelcome attention of the Slayers.

Depending on who hires the party, the wager for battling the knight can be changed from money to other rewards. One might be that, if the knight loses, he must remove his helm and reveal himself. He will agree to this wager only if the PC wagers at least 40 rilks or the little finger on their left hand. Collecting the finger may prove difficult for the knight if the rest of the party intervene, but if the wager was legally made, the city guard will step in on the knight's side and enforce payment.

The knight is indeed looking for a squire, or even a band of followers, to accompany him on a mission to Quarmall to discover the fate of his younger sister. The knight has a Strength score of 18/23 and a Dexterity score of 16. His plate armor is of poor quality and is equal only to chain mail (AC 4). The Wrestling Table on pages 97-98 of the *Player's Handbook* should be used to resolve any bout between the knight and a party member. The knight is a 7th-level chaotic good fighter with 62 hit points.

If the knight is forced to reveal himself, many are shocked to learn he is really a young woman—Recia of the noble family Ridoa. She is a tomboy and truly does want some help to find out what befell her sister. If she wins the bout and the PC stands to lose a finger, Recia will enlist the party's aid instead of exacting payment. She will only remove the finger if she has to force the PC to pay up and the PCs refuse to help her. If the party agree to help, payment is a matter for negotiation. There are no experience points or social levels gained or lost in the investigation.

Charles the Inventor

Tenderloin District

In the dim alleyways of the Tenderloin District is the home and workshop of Charles the inventor. A noble by birth, Charles is a remittance man. His family pays his rent on the condition that he never brings himself or his crackpot inventions to the family house, or show himself anywhere in the Noble District. Charles is fortunate to have his remittance, since he cannot remember the last time he sold one of his inventions. He even has trouble remembering when someone last came into his workshop.

Not one of his inventions has ever worked successfully, or at least, not the way he intended it to work. He built a water wheel that was supposed to lift water from the river into an irrigation ditch. Instead, it flung the water in all directions, soaking anyone who came near it. For a time, the wheel was used in the Festival District by small children, but eventually they grew tired of the game and it fell into disuse.

His plowshare was another unfortunate accident. Intended to cut deeper and wider than other ploughs, it instead dug into the ground and continued to dig, tunnelling under the fields. While it proved a good way to break up rocky soil and aerate old fields, the amount of effort involved was greater than the return. The same jobs could be done better and faster with more common tools.

Charles' most infamous invention was the self-sharpening sword. He built a scabbard with whetstones mounted inside it in an attempt to keep a sword sharp permanently. Charles' intent was that each time the sword was drawn or returned to the scabbard, it would be sharpened. Unfortunately, he forgot to account for the small filings that result from sharpening a sword. They collected in the bottom of the scabbard, and eventually they mixed with some blood and oil to dry and harden into a solid lump. While the lump was effective as a sling bullet, it required the scabbard to be pulled apart to remove it, and the owner cut himself badly on the whetstone strips when he dismantled the scabbard. Only Charles' noble status saved him from being run through by the few swordsmen who purchased his invention.

Charles is in his early thirties, and stands five feet one inch tall. He has short red curly hair and green eyes. He is reasonably fit, and weighs about 150 pounds. His one remaining link with his noble background is his dress. He always wears the finest clothes, and wears a peacock feather in any hat he dons.

A friendly fellow, Charles is always keen to talk to anyone who comes into his workshop. He has many inventions scattered around, all of which do something other than what he intended. He is willing to listen to people who want a specific tool or device. He becomes very serious, taking copious notes on their requirements, and nodding wisely at the right moments. After hearing what his customer wants, and agreeing on a fee which is always too low for what was requested, Charles promptly loses his notes and starts work from memory. This is his biggest problem.

Unfortunately, Charles has a memory like a sieve. He constantly "remembers" a customer specifying some detail that was really related to a project he started years ago. When something obviously doesn't fit the basic design, Charles changes the design so that everything fits. On any world but Nehwon, Charles would have been born a gnome.

Charles has tried several times to join the Artificers' Guild, but they have certain minimum standards which Charles is nowhere near meeting. Thus, he is one of the few in Lankhmar who is a freelancer and is not being pursued by the relevant guild to join up or face the consequences.

Every so often a new person in town buys one of Charles' inventions. More often than not, they prefer to pretend it didn't happen rather than admit how foolish they were to purchase one of Charles' contraptions. Some even put the inventions on display as "art", something which fools no one but gives the unfortunate purchaser an way to save face.

Very occasionally, one of Charles devices is actually useful, but it is never for what he intended. His mechanical stew stirrer didn't stop food from sticking to the bottom of the cooking pot, but it has proved useful as a skimmer in a number of whitesmiths' establishments. Of course, they would never admit where it came from, claiming to have bought it from a traveling tinker if pressed on the point.

A few weeks ago, a traveling merchant came to Charles and asked him to make a device that would screen a person from magical scrying. The device itself had to be nonmagical, but it had to render the wearer immune to scrying by any means.

Charles dutifully set to work to build the device, which was supposed to look like an ornamental torc. True to his usual form, Charles couldn't make the mechanics fit in a torc, so he made a helmet. It looked quite hideous with bits sticking out of it all over, but Charles was happy that he had made something for a paying customer. Perhaps now the Artificers would accept him.

Alas, when it came time to test the helmet, Charles discovered what he had built. He was trying it on for size, and he was overwhelmed by the voices which began all talking at once in his head. He quickly removed the helmet and, after collecting his wits, he began to analyze what had occurred. He quickly came to the conclusion that, rather than being a screen, the helmet caught and amplified the thoughts of nearby people, even through solid walls to the people in the streets outside.

Realizing the value of such a device, and the inherent danger of possessing it, he went straight to the Artificers for help. They took the device for testing and told him to come back the next day. If it worked, he would be admitted to the guild.

Charles has not been seen by anyone in Lankhmar since. The Artificers are concerned because they know how much membership of the guild meant to him and he should be around to hear their verdict.

Adventure Hooks

There are currently three interested parties looking for Charles. Firstly, the merchant who commissioned the torc wants to know when he can have his commissioned item.

Secondly, the Artificers are finally prepared to admit him to their ranks and he can't be found. In view of the importance of his invention, they are certain foul play has taken a hand. They are also concerned that the plans for the helmet will leave the city, and thus, their control. They would prefer to have the plans go into their guild library.

Thirdly, his family sent the monthly stipend along last evening, but Charles was not there. Ever since he left home, he has been waiting for his allowance each month without fail, even if he was ill. Although he is a black sheep, Charles is still a family member and there are concerns for his safety.

The party can be hired by one or more of these people to find Charles, or find out what happened to him. The merchant will pay 10 rilks for information, the Artificers will also pay 10 rilks, and the family will pay 20 rilks. The Artificers will not reveal what the device does, should the PCs ask.

Despite the confusion, the situation is simple: Charles got scared. Having finally built a device that worked, and such a potentially powerful device at that, he became worried that someone would try to steal it from him, or kill him, or both. So, he ran away and is staying in the Silver Eel under an assumed name. After two days in hiding, his curiosity will surface again and he will try to sneak home. He isn't very good at stealth, so he will be easy to catch. He will happily tell the party what he built once he is sure they mean him no harm.

Charles has no plans for the device, as that information is all in his head. Once the Artificers learn this, they will not release the helmet until one of their number has taken it apart and made schematics of it to duplicate.

Dricsal

Plaza and Tenderloin Districts

The town criers of Lankhmar are among the very few who can go anywhere in the city without fear of either attack or expulsion. They are able to carry messages between gangs or from criminals to city officials. They can also make general announcements in public places on behalf of the Overlord.

Dricsal is a town crier who wants to be something more. He has advanced as far as he can unless one of his superiors dies or leaves. He thinks that is unlikely, as none of them is very old and few people leave the ranks of the town criers willingly. It is, after all, an insurance policy as well as a license to snoop anywhere from the lowliest hovel in the Marsh District to the Overlord's Palace.

Dricsal wishes to find something that will not interfere with his life as a crier, but will bring a bit of spice into his life. He has made it known in some circles that he wants to become a thief, or at least an agent for some thieves. His current occupation makes him ideal as a spy for any group or individual.

Dricsal stands five feet seven inches tall and is slightly built. He dresses in foppish clothes, even when wearing his crier's tabard. Most people who know him consider him to be quite shallow and unintelligent. He is also considered effeminate by many, with his wide blue eyes, a feminine hair style, and a habitual vacuous expression only adds to this image.

Neither the Thieves' Guild nor Midnight's Band has a spy as effective (or as easily underestimated) as Dricsal could be, and both are interested in engaging his services once they check him out.

In current Lankhmar, all thieves' groups are wary of new recruits, always suspecting a plant from either the guild or Midnight. Even small freelance groups are being more careful about who they recruit, and this is making Dricsal very hot property that everybody wants but nobody is willing to take a chance on.

Dricsal's only real interest is Dricsal. He will work with anyone as long as they are useful to him, then cut himself free as cleanly as possible. He doesn't want people he's used seeking revenge on him, so he tries to make the break seem natural.

Adventure Hooks

Depending on who and what your PCs are, this could lead to several different approaches.

If they are members of the guild, Dricsal might approach them to sponsor his claim for employment or membership. Sponsorship involves the PC or PCs taking responsibility for the new recruit in all things, especially loyalty in these troubled times. If they agree to sponsor him, and Dricsal betrays the guild, the PCs will most likely be slain along with him. So, the PCs should assess his claim very carefully before agreeing.

As members of either the guild or Midnight's Band, the PCs can be asked to check out Dricsal's story and make sure he is available as a thief for the right group. Primarily, each group suspects Dricsal to be a plant of the other or of the Overlord.

If the PCs plan to start their own freelance thieving operation, perhaps Dricsal would be a useful contact for them. They should still want to check him out so they don't end up in a trap.

For whatever reason they are investigating Dricsal, what the PCs can find out is that he is genuinely interested in learning the ways of the thief, and that he doesn't particularly care who he works for.

His basic nature is not well suited to the politicking and bootlicking of the guild, but Dricsal would fit right in with Midnight's group or any freelancers with more interest in the right person for getting a job done than in who is owed a favor.

Money, experience and social levels will vary according to why this investigation is undertaken, but an increase in social level is unlikely in any event.

Falesh the Fortune Teller

Tenderloin District

Lankhmar, City of Sevenscore Thousand Smokes, is also the City of Sevenscore Thousand superstitions, or so it seems. Fortune tellers are as common as fleas on a dog in Lankhmar. For a few agols, they will read your future in a crystal ball, or cast a horoscope for the next month. Most of them are charlatans, but there are a few who have a genuine gift. Falesh is one of these authentic seers.

She is not a Lankhmart by birth, but came here from the Eastern Lands many years ago with a trade caravan. She liked the city and decided to stay for a time. As she has no inclination to leave, that time is likely to be the rest of her life.

Currently about thirty years old, Falesh has almond-colored eyes and shoulder length black hair. She wears a light veil in public, though it hides none of her beauty. There has been no shortage of men willing to court Falesh, for she is a truly beautiful and intelligent woman. Her eastern origins give her a certain mystical air, and she still dresses in the manner of the east, heightening the mystique.

Falesh is unmarried and has remained virtuous even in this city famous for its iniquity. To lose her virginity would be to lose her gift, or so she was taught by her mother. True fortune tellers must remain chaste until they are ready to forfeit their seers' gifts, have children, and pass on their talents to the next generation. As Falesh has yet to meet a man she is willing to spend the rest of her life with, she has remained chaste.

She has a small shop and apartment on Shady Street where she tells fortunes for a minimum fee of one smerduk. As her fortunes are generally accurate, her customers do not object to paying a little more for her work. She uses a crystal ball because most of her customers expect it, but it is not a necessary part of her work. Neither are the cards she uses for more detailed fortunes. The only thing Falesh needs to tell someone's fortune is to have them close enough to touch. As long as she remains in contact with a person, she can generally tell what will befall them in the next day, week, or month. It is possible to guess the future beyond a month, but it is not reliable. Falesh always warns customers about long range predictions, as she believes in giving value for money.

Because she must touch someone to tell anything about their future, Falesh is not useful as a tool in locating missing persons, or even to tell whether a person is still alive. She can sometimes get this information indirectly, by looking for whether her customer will soon be reunited with the missing person, or may be attending a funeral for them. This line of scrying is unreliable at best, though.

Sometimes Falesh does not wish to reveal what she has seen, such as an imminent death of a customer. She will not lie to them if asked directly, but she will often tell a half truth or skirt around the issue if the customer doesn't press the point.

Adventure Hooks

Many adventuring companies use Falesh to determine whether a commission they have been offered is going to be profitable, or to check if there might be something about a job their employer hasn't told them. Falesh charges three smerduks for this service, which is quite reasonable since she must tell the fortune of each member of a group. Of course, an adventure may be profitable for the group, but at the cost of one or more members' lives. As she explains to all her customers, it is her policy to reveal only that a mission will succeed or not. She will never identify those marked for death, since such knowledge would alter the group outcome with PCs who suddenly wouldn't go. She explains this before taking her fee.

If the characters are regular customers, Falesh is looking for someone to take her to Tisilinilit for a short visit so she can look for a mate and send a message home to her family. She is not expecting trouble, but does not believe in taking unnecessary risks. Falesh wants to travel with people she knows and trusts, not strangers.

Fredoa

Plaza District

In the Plaza and Festival Districts of Lankhmar, there are many entertainers, most of whom work the street corners hoping to make enough money to eat. The talented or lucky ones get permanent jobs in troupes. One who receives offers for positions in several professional troupes, but always refuses as she waits for "a better offer," is Fredoa the singer.

Fredoa is of medium build, with pretty features and a ready smile. Her shoulder-length blonde hair is sometimes tied back in a bun but it flows around her face far more often. She is never short of an audience, or of male company, if she wants it.

Fredoa spends more time in the Plaza District than most singers and, combined with her better-than-average talents, the lack of competition ensures a reasonable income. She is often found in or near the Plaza of Dark Delights, but rarely after dark. Fredoa is self confident but not to the point of needless risk.

She lives in the Rising Moon tavern, and is one of only a few who use its rooms for sleep. As it is in the Tenderloin District, and Fredoa is both pretty and diminutive, she doesn't like to be out after dark. Many of her evenings are spent in the taproom, entertaining the guests while they drink. In lieu of payment for the entertainment, Fredoa gets her room and two meals a day free of charge. It's a cozy arrangement that works well for both Fredoa and Tamol the innkeeper.

The choice of residence was influenced by the nocturnal visitors Fredoa sometimes gets. There are so many comings and goings at the Rising Moon that no one notices if someone goes upstairs to Fredoa's room.

Fredoa is a member of the Society of Joyous and Sorrowful Comedians, Rapturous Playactors, Graceful Dancers, and Melodious Songsters, but not due to any need or measure of guild loyalty. She is a member only because she would be hounded by the Society, or some hired thugs, to join or get out of Lankhmar. She is not popular with other singers, both because she chooses to work in strange parts of the city, and because she is a better singer and entertainer than most of the other Society singers. Such jealousies are quite common in Lankhmar, as they are in any world, and Fredoa has a number of enemies in the Society, most notably Andrea, the current lover of the Society's leader.

Despite her income from singing, it is her other career that nets Fredoa most of her hidden wealth. She is a scout for the infamous thief, Midnight. Fredoa often checks out prospective new members to Midnight's band, or watches a target to spot Thieves' Guild observers. She uses the subtle technique of being so obvious about her presence at any location that nobody pays any attention to her. To keep her association with Midnight a secret, any raids on areas cased by Fredoa are held over for two to five nights after her singing session in the area.

Fredoa became a scout for Midnight because she found her life boring. Doing nothing but singing all day, `singing for her supper' she often called it, became tedious and Fredoa craved something more. She dabbled with picking pockets but the risk of being caught far outweighed any thrill of success. The money she stole was never a major factor in her decision. It was the challenge she was after.

Eventually Fredoa was spotted picking a pocket—fortunately, not by the pocket's owner. She was contacted by one of Midnight's agents and asked if she would like to act as a scout. This was just what she'd always wanted. It gave her the thrill of being something other than what she seemed, and provided her the opportunity to take from those who could afford the loss. Finally, the security of a regular income free of guild interference was too good to miss.

She enjoys the chance to recruit new members for Midnight, recalling the shock of being caught out when she was first contacted. She likes watching people squirm and stutter as they try to deny their thieving activities or their disaffection with the Thieves' Guild.

Adventure Hooks

Someone has threatened Fredoa's life. It could be a rival singer, or maybe the Thieves' Guild has finally caught on to her extra activities. The player characters are required to keep Fredoa alive until the source of the threat is identified and neutralized.

The pay is 10 agols per guard per day. Although Fredoa is handing over the money, it is, in reality, coming from Midnight. After three days of relative boredom, while Fredoa cases the Thieves' guild house in the Tenderloin District, a trio of agents from the Slayers' Brotherhood will attack Fredoa on her way to the Rising Moon tavern. Each of the Slayers is armed with a short sword and a poisoned dagger. They have one attack each per round, dealing 1-6 points of damage with short swords or 1-4 points plus poison damage with the daggers (save vs. poison or die in 1-10 rounds). Each Slayer has a THAC0 of 18, AC 9, and 12 hit points. Killing or capturing the Slayers will gain the party 375 XP. Driving them off will gain 250 XP. A bonus of 300 XP can be had if the PCs question any prisoners and find out who hired them. They were hired by Andrea, another singer, who is insanely jealous of Fredoa's talents and who heard rumors that Fredoa was stealing Andrea's lover (Not true). In either case, all party members who actually take part in the combat will gain a social level, at least temporarily.

They may also bring the wrath of the Slayers' Brotherhood down upon themselves, at the DM's option. If the party members are defeated and survive, the experience awarded should be no more than 125 XP. If any cowardice was shown in the combat, a loss of one social level, at least temporarily, may be appropriate.

Assuming the characters keep Fredoa alive, they will shortly be contacted by one of Midnight's agents to see if they want to join her growing band. Midnight is not keen on taking "no" for an answer and may try to eliminate any player characters that won't ally with her.

Jendar

Plaza District

The City of Adventure has a new tenant—Jendar the Ilthmart. Jendar came to Lankhmar five days ago as a merchant, and took a room at the Wooden Leg. Four days ago, a priest of the Rat God appeared in the Plaza of Dark Delights preaching doom to the worshippers of the false gods, and claiming the ascendancy of the Rat God was nigh.

Crazy priests are not uncommon in Lankhmar and they usually go away after an hour or two if everyone ignores them. Jendar is different. He stayed in the Plaza, haranguing everyone with his tales of woe to the unbelievers, until some of the merchants complained to the city guards that he was affecting their business. The guards moved him on, but he was back next day. Overnight, he had been evicted from the Wooden Leg and had moved into the Rat God's temple with the other priests.

Undaunted by his eviction or the city guard, Jendar again began preaching the ways of his god to all and sundry, heedless of the unpopularity of the Rat God in Lankhmar.

Some folk in the Plaza are beginning to suspect that Jendar is not what he seems. He must be doing this to distract people while an accomplice snatches their purse or steals from their stall. There can be no other rational explanation for his behavior.

Since Jendar is not rational, his behavior isn't either. In truth, he has no accomplice and is genuinely trying to promote his god and convert unbelievers before the day of ascendancy arrives. He is higher in his church's hierarchy than any of the local priests, so they cannot take any action to dissuade him, even though they realize the damage he is doing to their cause.

Jendar is a gaunt man, with rodentlike features that have obviously been the result of surgery combined with magic. The scars where his nose and cheekbones were altered will never heal, and the lines around his eyes puff up in red sores most mornings.

This is quite a cunning disguise on Jendar's part. By making it seem like he deliberately and rather crudely altered his features, it doesn't occur to anyone that Jendar might actually have some rat blood in him, or that he might be a wererat. He is a wererat, and like most of his kind, he detests his human form.

However, he is crafty enough to realize that a Rat God priest with rodentlike features that seem natural would be set upon as a wererat in any city outside Ilthmar. So, he disfigured himself and he rubs an irritant in his eyes each morning to get the puffiness up before he goes into the street. It wears off in a few hours, and is nowhere near as painful as it looks.

Jendar has been to Lankhmar Below each evening since his arrival, and has gained the confidence of the local wererats and their giant rat cousins. He is powerful enough to summon every rat in a 200 yard radius if he chooses to do so. He has not yet told the rats or the priests why he is here, but as the Vermin Day "celebration" is only six days off, it is almost certain his plans have something to do with that day.

Apart from his preaching in the Plaza, Jendar has been berating passersby in the street as he goes to and from the temple, and he has dropped into several shops to preach loudly to the owners and their customers. In each of these shops, Jendar has been physically removed by the owner or the city guard, but not until he has scared off many of the customers.

What few Lankhmarts realize, and one of the reasons for Jendar's odd behavior, is that each of the shops he visited is run by a secret worshipper of the Rat God, and Jendar wanted to scare off the customers so he could have a private chat with the proprietor.

Jendar and his followers are planning an attack on Vermin Day. The ghouls may well attack at the same time if they haven't been discovered, and an Ilthmart force as well if Sheldon got back with her report. (See page 41 for more information.) Vermin Day will indeed be very busy in the City of Sevenscore Thousand Smokes this year.

Adventure Hooks

Come the Vermin Day festival, the worshipers of the Rat God (and others) will make their move. Most of the activity will be around The Pit in the River District. There will be other activities going on elsewhere, including what the Rat God's followers regard as the barbaric custom of selling rat-on-a-stick to the humans.

While many Lankhmarts are at The Pit, Jendar and his followers plan to emerge from Lankhmar Below and capture the Plaza of Dark Delights. They figure they can wreak havoc in the relatively quiet Plaza and return to the tunnels before the militia can react.

Jendar expects the city to retaliate by sending patrols into the tunnels to hunt down and kill hundreds, or even thousands, of rats. He plans to ambush these patrols and to eradicate the humans a few at a time. He also expects the ghouls to be keeping a number of the city guard and militia busy.

So, the PCs can become involved in this battle on either side. If they are worshippers of the Rat God and are known to the priests, Jendar will contact them and give them their orders about which tunnels in Lankhmar Below are their responsibility.

If they are not worshipers, they will be called upon by the city, along with all free adventuring companies, to join the hunt for the rats in the sewers and tunnels.

It is even possible the PCs could be in the Plaza when the attack begins, and they could be among the first to be attacked. Defeating the initial assault would be a major blow to Jendar's plans. Between 150 and 200 rats will attack the Plaza, led by five wererats and Jendar. Jendar is AC 6, has 31 hit points, and a THAC0 of 16. He will fight to the death if cornered.

If the party encounters rats in the tunnels, there will be 21-40 rats, plus one wererat. Jendar will only be encountered in the tunnels if more than 500 rats have been killed by the party. Due to the huge numbers of rats and other foes in this scenario, this adventure scenario is not recommended for player characters below 9th level.

Jermat the Black Wizard

Tenderloin District

Jermat the Black Wizard lives in a splendid apartment just off Damp Street, surrounded by arcane symbols and tomes of magical spells and potions.

Jermat is horribly disfigured due to his magic. On the rare occasions he is seen in public, he wears black robes with a heavy cowl pulled down over his face. He always looks down toward his feet and he doesn't take kindly to folk stepping in his way. His response to someone blocking his path is usually a *magic missile* or a *lightning bolt* from his wand (if he is in a really foul mood).

As his features are always hidden in public, Jermat's age is unknown, as are his distinguishing features. He must be at least 40 years old since he has had his apartment for nearly 20 years and some folk dimly remember the fresh faced young man who took the apartment way back then.

Jermat is now a 13th-level black wizard and he has an impressive collection of spellbooks. He also has at least eleven magical wands. He carries six of these in a bandolier under his robes, where he can quickly grab whichever one he wants. While his collection of magical items is not the largest in Lankhmar, it is certainly significant. At any time, Jermat is likely to have his *wand of lightning bolts*, a *wand of magic missiles*, a *wand of sleep*, a magically-returning *winged dagger*, a *wand of ice storm*, and a *wand of defoliation* in his bandolier. He is rumored to possess a *wand of wonder*, but this is unconfirmed as the only person foolish enough to ask him about it did not live to report the answer.

Having spent many years researching magic and stealing other wizard's spellbooks to copy into his own, Jermat has the following spells available to him. Those marked with an asterisk (*) are the ones he habitually memorizes.

Level One—*audible glamer, burning hands, chill touch**, *color spray, detect magic, enlarge, hypnotism**, *hold portal, identify, magic missile**, *protection from good, read magic, reduce, shocking grasp, sleep**, *ventriloquism, wall of fog**

Level Two—*bind, blindness**, *darkness 15' radius, flaming sphere, forget**, *invisibility**, *ray of enfeeblement, stinking cloud**, *web**, *wizard lock*

Level Three—*clairaudience, clairvoyance, dispel magic, fireball**, *fly, hold person**, *lightning bolt**, *slow, suggestion**, *wraithform**

Level Four—*bestow curse**, *confusion**, *detect scrying, fear**, *ice storm**, *polymorph other, polymorph self, remove curse, wizard eye*

Level Five—*cloudkill, cone of cold**, *contact other plane, dismissal, domination, magic jar, major creation, passwall, telekinesis, teleport**

When he was younger, Jermat fell in love with a bootmaker's daughter. She was very beautiful, and caught the eye of many young men. Determined to woo her, Jermat put all his time and energy into impressing her, but to no avail. She ran off with an adventuring company and was killed in a battle with some ghouls. Jermat was devastated and swore a vow of hatred against all male adventurers. He also vowed to go barefoot for the rest of his life.

Since taking up his current residence, Jermat has killed at least two adventuring companies (a total of thirteen people).

Adventure Hooks

PCs will find Jermat nearly impossible to engage, save as a powerful adversary. He is likely to kill any male adventurer who approaches him, and females are also hard pressed to employ him. If a group confronts him, he will attack everyone all at once.

He is susceptible to offers of magical items he doesn't have or spellbooks containing spells he doesn't know. Rare or expensive spell components can also help PCs to get a foot in Jermat's door. Simple money, however, means nothing to Jermat.

Once he agrees to aid a party, Jermat will do his utmost to fulfil his end of the deal and he expects his employers to do the same. A mixed party of males and females should keep the men well away from Jermat. He will not kill them once he has agreed to help, but neither will he be friendly towards them. Once the job is done, Jermat takes his payment and leaves. He will attempt to slay PCs who deceive him.

Lamit the Storyteller

Plaza District

At the eastern end of the Plaza of Dark Delights, near the Fountain of Dark Abundance, residents and travelers gather to listen to the storyteller named Lamit.

Lamit is an excellent wordsmith, and she makes a reasonable income from her listeners' donations. She doesn't make enough to finance her wardrobe, but she does clear enough to live comfortably in the lower-class areas of the city.

She seems to have an endless wardrobe. Her regular listeners cannot remember ever seeing her wear the same outfit twice, although she has been known to wear the same cut of clothing in two or more different colors.

Like all the well known entertainers in Lankhmar, Lamit is a member of the Society of Joyous and Sorrowful Comedians, Rapturous Playactors, Graceful Dancers, and Melodious Songsters. She has had some trouble with senior members wanting to know why she won't work the Festival District like most of her brethren, but Lamit is adamant that the Plaza is the only place she will work. Ultimately, the Society is happy simply to collect her dues and many fellow members are relieved to not have to compete with her for their income in the Festival District.

A slight woman of just over five feet, Lamit's blue eyes always seem to be looking right through every person in her audience. She has long brown hair, which is sometimes done up in a tight bun but largely falls freely to her waist.

A feature of Lamit's storytelling which her regulars know to look for is the tone of the day's stories. If a person knows what to look for, they can tell what's in store for the day by the color and cut of Lamit's clothing:

- a dress means the story will be romantic;
- a skirt and blouse suggest a tale of darkness and evil;
- breeches means that high adventure is the topic for the day;
- soft colors such as blue or green foreshadow a sad ending or an odd twist in the plot;
- bright colors such as red and yellow mean the story will have a violent end; and
- drab colors such as gray, brown, and black lead to the downfall of the heroes and victory for the forces of darkness.

Unlike her wardrobe, Lamit's stories do get used more than once. She has a repertoire of around 150 stories, and she sometimes varies the telling and even the ending of a story to keep even her most avid listeners in suspense.

In spite of her ability, Lamit is not a true bard. She cannot sing or play a single note. However, many of Nehwon's bards come to listen to Lamit's stories, then put them to music in their own fashion, adding to their own personal repertoires. Most bards acknowledge Lamit as their source for tales of adventure and romance, and more than one has told a new tale of the storyteller by the fountain.

Lankhmar is a city where material for stories is plentiful, so it is hardly a surprise that many of Lamit's stories feature a giant barbarian and his diminutive companion. Fafhrd and the Gray Mouser are a godsend to all bards and wordsmiths, and Lamit is particularly skilful at making these scoundrels seem like folk heroes to the ordinary citizens of Lankhmar.

When darkness falls and the Plaza takes on a more sinister air, Lamit continues her storytelling for a few hours before returning to her home. Nobody bothers her as she is considered harmless and a fine entertainer. Besides, storytellers and bards are protected in Lankhmar (as in other cities and other worlds) by the unwritten law that permits the bringers of entertainment and news safety in the most dangerous situations.

Lamit's home is something of a mystery to her many fans. She has been followed from the Plaza countless times, but always manages to lose her pursuers up around the twisting alleyways of the Tenderloin District. Her route is never the same two nights running, so even those clever enough to wait for her where they lost her last are unable to pick up her trail. A few folk who were sure they had found her home have disappeared.

The reason for Lamit's secrecy is that she is a noblewoman, a baroness, who is very close to the Overlord. She is a master of disguise and her appearance as Lamit the storyteller is very different from her real self. Her name really is Lamit, but that is not an uncommon name in Lankhmar. She has short black hair, and her brown hair is actually several wigs in a number of different styles. She stands just an inch short of five feet, and she wears special shoes to make Lamit the Storyteller seem taller.

Her true work in the Plaza is really done in the last few hours of darkness before she goes home. The Overlord wants to know what is happening in the nighttime markets of the Plaza, but any overt investigations are spotted quickly and cause most of the traders to pack up until the guards or hired investigators have left. Lamit, by staying around all day, is not an object of distrust, and she picks up quite a lot of information about the goings-on in the Plaza. Her reports to the Overlord are always delivered in person at social functions, using a private code only she and the Overlord understand. So, when guests at a party hear the Overlord and Lamit discussing the latest fashions, they have no idea that their ruler is being informed of a shipment of virulent poison that arrived that week, bound for the members of the Slayers' Brotherhood.

Lamit agreed to become a spy for the Overlord many years ago, as a personal favor to him, and because it sounded far more exciting than life in high society. She originally intended to spy for only a short time in the hopes to win the Overlord's hand. She quickly decided that being a spy was far more interesting than being a wife and mother, even if the wife and mother was Lankhmar's first lady.

Adventure Hooks

An anonymous employer wants to know about Lamit's private life. A fee of 250 rilks will be paid for information about where she lives, and why she is so secretive about her private life. The employer will not identify himself and will always be dressed in concealing clothing when the PCs meet him. The payment will be 50 rilks up front, and the balance is received by the PCs upon delivery of the information.

The employer is a senior member of the Thieves' Guild. The guild members want to know about Lamit, as they suspect she is working for Midnight. One or two thieves have even suggested Lamit may actually be Midnight, but that is not taken seriously by the misogynistic leaders of the guild. The guild has tried many times to find Lamit's secret, but each time the thief or thieves sent out came back empty handed, or did not come back at all.

A clever party will take the commission from their mysterious employer, then confront Lamit in the Plaza. If she is told of the interest in her private life, she will politely thank the PCs, and ask them to bring their employer along to the corner of Bones Alley and Plague Court the next evening to show him where she lives.

If the PCs turn up with the thief, they will be ambushed by the Overlord's personal guards in tattered clothing. The thief/employer will be killed, and the PCs will be told they need to look like they were in a pitched battle to protect themselves from retaliation by the guild. If they agree, the guards will rough up the party, doing no permanent or serious damage, and leave them. If they do not agree, the guards will attempt to kill the party. Each guard is armed with a broad sword, and has chain mail under his outer garments. They have a THAC0 of 14, 38 hit points each, and do 2-8 points of damage per hit. They attack only once each per round. Each guard is worth 280 XP if defeated or killed.

Martin the White Wizard

Tenderloin District

Among the more eccentric residents of the Tenderloin District is Martin the White Wizard. Martin lives alone in an apartment on Damp Street, surrounded by bits of plants and several staves that are probably magical in nature, but nobody knows exactly what magic they contain.

He is of indeterminate age, seeming about 30, but he has looked like he does now for the last ten years and will likely do so for the next ten as well. He is slightly built and he walks with a stoop when he walks at all.

Unlike most white wizards, Martin wanders the streets in the daytime, rushing from place to place and not watching where he is going. It is up to others to keep out of his way as he dislikes being bumped into. Any collision between Martin and a person, animal, or building is always the other's fault. They bumped into him, never the other way around. No one cares to ask him how a building could suddenly leap in front of him, as it would be too risky.

Martin is quite insane. Though he claims to be a great wizard, he has seldom been seen casting a spell, because he lacks the necessary attention span for anything even a little complex and certainly does not exhibit the patience required to relearn a spell, once cast. Nevertheless, he has a reputation as a powerful wizard in the Tenderloin District. The spells he does cast never seem to have any immediately visible effect, but if he says he has cast a spell to cause something to happen, or to stop something happening, his predictions tend to come true within a day.

Rumor has it that Martin can cast any spell he chooses, perhaps with the help of one of his staves to focus his attention. This rumor cannot be entirely true since Death has decreed that no *raise dead* or *resurrection* spells can work on the world of Nehwon.

In actuality, Martin is a complete fraud. He cannot cast a single spell of either white or black magic. Much of his "magic" is the simple suggestion of "charms" and "curses." Since he has a reputation as a great wizard, many believe the "spells" to be true and often unconsciously cause them to happen.

Martin is not totally without magic, however. He does possess a magical staff that can act as a conduit to Votishal. Martin has learned that the god only grants requests that aid its worshipers. Martin, therefore, frames his few "spells" accordingly. As he is not strictly a priest of Votishal, he is not required to be of lawful good alignment, nor to be a thief. Martin is of Chaotic Good alignment, and would never "cast" a spell that would harm a living creature, even if he were a real white wizard.

Adventure Hooks

Dealing with wizards, even white ones, is fraught with danger for mundane folk. Few can fathom the workings of a wizard's mind, and many unwary visitors to a wizard's abode have come away changed into frogs, or worse. Still, there are times when a wizard's services are needed. Finding a missing person or valuable heirloom, healing a companion or family member when the Physicians cannot help, or warding off extraplanar creatures are tasks only for those who wield magic.

Martin's services are particularly difficult to engage, since he has to know exactly what's required before he can take a commission. Healing is possible, but only if the patient is a thief of a non-evil alignment. Combat spells are definitely out, and Martin explains this by claiming to have a taboo against killing anyone.

Martin charges a minimum of twenty rilks for any service, and his normal fee is fifteen rilks per level of the "spell" he is required to cast.

Rondal the Beastmaster

Plaza District

Most members of the Animal Handlers' Guild are common folk who deal with teams of draft animals, bulls, horses and the like. Rondal the beastmaster is different.

He has a large piece of real estate on the outside wall of the Plaza District, just off Wall Street. There are four large buildings that make up Rondal's business.

Rondal himself is a giant of a man, and he certainly has some barbarian blood in him. He stands six feet nine inches tall in bare feet and wears thick heavy boots that give him an extra inch of height. He has a bushy red beard and often looks quite fearsome. His normal garb consists of soft trousers and a sheepskin coat. He always carries a whip at his side and a quarterstaff strapped to his back for his work with the animals.

His wife and two sons help out with the business, but only Rondal trains the animals he sells. His elder son, Montal, is learning to train the animals. Montal is 14 years old and is a smaller version of his father, and he lacks his father's beard. He is just over six feet tall and still growing. Rondal chose him to learn the trade not because he was the firstborn, but because he showed an affinity for the animals and that is very necessary for a beastmaster.

The Nehwon beastmaster is not the same as the AD&D NPC class. Like Nehwon priests, the term beastmaster is just a description of their occupation and conveys no special abilities. The beastmaster, for lack of better examples, is part ranger, part druid, and part circus trainer. A beastmaster controls and trains animals using a mixture of trust and rewards with the occasional punishment.

Rondal's second son, Lartal, is ten years old and does most of the menial work around the business. He cleans out the cages, and parades the smaller animals for prospective buyers. He also helps his mother with the house. Lartal has told his family he wants to become a famous adventurer, like the Gray Mouser. Given his heritage, Rondal has suggested that he is more likely to mimic Fafhrd than the Mouser, if he doesn't end up on the wrong end of a hangman's noose. Rondal is certain Lartal will grow out of his notions of heroic adventures throughout the lands, but his mother and brother aren't so sure.

Rondal's wife, Leena, is a small woman who is dwarfed even by her youngest son Lartal. She has little to do with the selling, and no part at all in the training of the animals, as she doesn't really like the idea of forcing a living creature to do unnatural things. She has brought the subject up several times with Rondal, but he always assures her the animals are not being asked to do anything unnatural, but only to use their full potential. Leena is unconvinced, but is holding her tongue for now.

There is a groundswell of support in Lankhmar for animal rights, something the Overlord and the Animal Handlers' Guild were quick to denounce as a trick by the rats to get rights and establish a foothold in the city again. While it is true the rats would benefit from animal rights, most of the activists are humans. A very small number of them are genuinely concerned about the welfare of all living things, but these few idealists are outnumbered by those who see it as just another way to stir up trouble and turn a profit from picking pockets.

Most beastmasters stick to training war dogs and the occasional leopard as well as monkeys and birds. Rondal has a reputation for training any animal that's ever been brought to him. He is known to have trained wolves, wolverns, giant crocodiles, marsh leopards, and once he even trained a carrion crawler. The more challenging the job, the more Rondal charges for the training. It is rumored he sold the carrion crawler for four gluditches, but this is unconfirmed. No one except Rondal knows who bought the crawler or why they bought it.

The northernmost of the four buildings Rondal and his family occupy is their home. It is a comfortable two-story house with three bedrooms, a kitchen, and common room used for eating and entertaining. In winter, a fire is kept burning all day and night in the common room.

The next building is the sales room where fully trained animals are sold or put through their paces for a client. There are several cages at the back of this building, mostly empty. Few of Rondal's animals remain unsold for long. There are also two pits for holding those animals that bars don't bother or are too big for a cage. The building is two stories high, but the second floor has been removed and bleachers have been put in to allow up to 60 people to sit and watch the animals.

The third building backs onto the city wall and is used to house animals undergoing training. It is heavily barred outside and the cages are all reinforced with extra bars. There is only one floor, plus a couple of pits for the crocodiles and any snakes Rondal may be training.

The last building is the training house. It has a central courtyard where most of the training takes place. The four wings of the building contain barred rooms where animals can exercise or do minor training. These rooms are also used when the weather prohibits training outdoors.

At any time, Rondal can have up to twenty animals undergoing training. Some will be almost ready to be returned to their owners or sold to the highest bidder. Others will still be getting used to life in captivity, not yet in formal training, and very dangerous. Most are somewhere in between the two extremes, although even the trained ones can be dangerous to anyone other than Rondal.

Adventure Hooks

- A rare Ice Cat is being sold to the highest bidder and Rondal fears some of the animal activists will try to disrupt the auction. He has hired the PCs to ensure that doesn't happen. Alternatively, the PCs could be the activists who wish to stop this "barbaric" behavior on Rondal's part. As a third option, they may wish to purchase the cat either for themselves or for an anonymous employer.

- The party has captured a young gladiator lizard and wants Rondal to train it for them. He is willing to try, but offers no guarantees as the lizard is more intelligent than any creature Rondal has trained in the past. He knows that, if he can succeed, his reputation will be enhanced by being the first (and only) person ever to train a gladiator lizard. Even so, he will want a lot of money if he succeeds, at least three gluditches. He will want one gluditch in advance, whether he is ultimately successful or not.

- The PCs are about to set off on a dangerous mission where the services of a particular animal would be helpful. Rondal is the most likely person in town to have what they want, from a spider monkey to another carrion crawler. What he has on hand at any time is wildly variable, depending on the supply of wild animals and the time taken to train them. There should be no more than a 50% chance of the PCs getting the trained animal they want. That chance may be further reduced if they want a rare or special creature.

- A number of Rondal's untrained animals have escaped, killing his son Lartal in the process. The city guard has been called to eliminate the creatures before they kill anyone else. Rondal would prefer them recaptured as they are quite valuable. The PCs can be part of the hunt, paid by the guards or by Rondal, or both.

Rongark the Water Carrier

Tenderloin District

In a port city with so much water nearby, it is surprising how little of it is fresh. Pure, clean drinking water is one of the rarest liquids in Lankhmar, and those who want it certainly pay heavily for it.

Rongark is a water carrier, a man who goes out into the Great Marsh in search of springs or pools of clear, pure water. It is not a difficult task, since the marsh has many clean springs once you get away from the city. However, it becomes dangerous farther away from the city. The creatures in the marsh do not like having their territory invaded by the many-headed beasts with huge bodies—the horses and wagon—nor do they like the small creatures that accompany the monster, except as their next meal.

It is the danger in obtaining the water that makes it so expensive. Most folk just use the brackish water from the wells, but as time goes on and more refuse from the city finds its way into the Hlal and the sea, the brackish water is becoming more and more tainted. More and more, people are paying for pure water to drink.

Rongark and the other water carriers have several permanent customers—the brewers in Lankhmar. Tainted water makes tainted beer and ale, and patrons won't drink it. So, the brewers buy pure water to keep their products marketable.

Rongark works with his two sons, each man taking a turn at pumping water into the huge barrel on the wagon while the other two stand guard. It takes three hours to fill the barrel, and the trip to the springs is two hours out and three back with the loaded wagon.

From a distance, they look like triplets. Each man is almost six feet tall, and broad shouldered. They have identical builds and each has a shock of black hair and a bushy beard. Only from close quarters can Rongark be identified from his sons. He hides his age well, and the beard helps that, but he does have a few heavy wrinkles around the corners of his eyes.

Rongark is a hearty person, being quite friendly and prepared to look for the good points in anyone he meets. This earnestness and honesty has sometimes cost him, as con men and cheats take advantage of him, but he is quite wealthy and is canny enough that he never loses a lot of money.

In three weeks, Rongark's only daughter, Rucelda, comes of age. In celebration, and in the hope of finding a suitable husband for her, Rongark is throwing a party at his house. All of Rucelda's friends have been invited, as have all the eligible bachelors Rongark could find among the nobility and the clergy. There are rumors that even the Overlord and his family are attending. It promises to be a major event on the social calendar, and certainly bigger than anything the Tenderloin District has seen for many years. The caterers have been given their instructions, the entertainment has been arranged, and one of Rongark's customers is providing the beverages from his brewery.

Such preparations do not go unnoticed in other circles. Such a gathering of wealthy folk outside the Citadel is a prime target for kidnapers, or a grand plan to take over Rongark's place and hold all the occupants for ransom. The successful execution of a plot of that magnitude would allow the perpetrators to take their money and live comfortably for the rest of their lives, provided they fled far from Lankhmar to avoid the vengeance of their victims. As Rongark is such a trusting person, the thought of anyone ruining his daughter's party has not occurred to him.

Rucelda is very beautiful, with long black hair as fine as silk, and sparkling brown eyes that always seem to be laughing. She is not as naive as her father, but puts on a show for him as she loves him dearly. She knows the real reason for the party, and is a little sad, as she has no wish to be wed to some foppish noble who wants her only for her family's money or to ensure that his family bloodline is secure. She wants a life first, and a family later. If the chance to run off with a handsome adventurer presents itself, she will jump at it if she can avoid hurting her father.

Adventure Hooks

Although Rongark is naive about the possibility of the party being disrupted, many of the guests are not. A number of nobles who have been the victims of previous kidnapings or hostage situations are planning to bring guards with them and station them around the property in case of trouble. If the Overlord does come (DM's choice), he will certainly have his elite personal guard with him.

Members of the Extortionists' Guild plan to kidnap several guests from the party, and ransom them back to their families. Rucelda herself is one of their prime targets. The plan is fairly simple—go in and grab whoever is close, then get out quickly. With so many wealthy people in one place, there are few specific targets. The Overlord and his family are definitely not targets, as they are always too well protected (and the possible repercussions for the guild too costly).

The PCs can be hired as additional guards by a guest to watch for trouble. On the flip side, they may be hired as the kidnapers. If they've been hired to keep someone safe, their first duty is to their employer, although they may help other people if it does not endanger their employer. With so many guards stationed in the streets around the property, the biggest danger is that some of them will get slack, and expect someone else's guards to keep their eyes open. This is what the extortionists are counting on to allow them to get in and out without too much trouble. Only the Overlord's guards will be constantly alert, and they'll be inside at the party.

Since Rucelda wants a life of adventure more than a husband, one or more PCs could be guests at the party, and offer to let her join their adventuring band. If she gets a decent offer, Rucelda will agree to sneak out the next day and run off with the band. She has very nimble fingers and could be trained as a thief, or as an archer if one is needed. She is good with animals, so she could become a ranger if someone can train her. Other classes are possible, but Rucelda would not adapt to them as readily, and she will never become a black wizard.

Sheldon

Tenderloin District

Sheldon is a courtesan from Ilthmar. Like many natives of that city, she worships the Rat God, although she will not do so openly while she is in Lankhmar.

Sheldon is quite beautiful and is much sought after in her home city as an escort to formal occasions as well as the more tawdry duties of a more common courtesan. She stands a little over five feet tall and has jet-black hair that falls almost to her waist. Her green eyes sparkle with an inner light that speaks of someone who knows more than she lets on. Sheldon is always busy and her appointment calendar is filled three to four months in advance.

Sheldon claims to have come to Lankhmar for a vacation. She needed to get away from Ilthmar since her high profile made it almost impossible to find any time to call her own. There are many in Lankhmar who do not believe her, including the Red Lanterns for starters.

Since her arrival two days ago, Sheldon has done some shopping in the Plaza, gone to the Festival District to see what was happening, gone to see some couturiers (dressmakers) in the Mercantile district, and spent her evenings at the Silver Eel. She has not mixed with the other patrons of that infamous tavern, preferring to take her meals in the taproom and then retire to her room for some privacy.

Her behavior has sparked much interest and has been the topic of several taproom conversations. Everyone who drinks at the Silver Eel is sure they know why Sheldon is here and why she is behaving like a recluse. Of course, everyone has a different story to tell, and each teller is certain "I'm the one truly in the know about this. . . . ".

Sheldon has not escaped the direct attention of the male customers in the Eel, but she has surprisingly rebuffed all advances toward her. Still, the Red Lanterns are sure she is up to no good, at least as they see and understand the situation.

The Rat God priests know that Sheldon has another purpose in coming to Lankhmar. She is bringing them news and a special delivery from

Ilthmar. What they do not understand is why she has not yet been to see them. They believed she would come to them immediately upon arriving in Lankhmar. They are curious about the delay, though they are not yet concerned that anything is wrong.

The Vermin Catchers' Guild suspects that Sheldon has a sinister purpose in Lankhmar. This surprises no one, since they always suspect all Ilthmarts of having a sinister purpose, unless they are specifically known not to worship the Rat God.

A number of Lankhmar's single men (and a few married ones who fancy themselves lady killers) are interested in Sheldon, too. There are rumors of sizeable bets among the men as to which one of them will gain Sheldon as an escort first. The simple answer to that bet is none of them. Sheldon has several reasons for not wanting any liaisons while she is in Lankhmar. Firstly, she really is taking a vacation from that part of her life while she is on the Rat God's mission. Secondly, if she did agree to go out with one of the men, it would only start a line at her door, and the Red Lanterns would get more annoyed than they already are (and the Lanterns are watching Sheldon constantly).

What even the local Rat God priests do not know is that Sheldon is here to explore and learn the city for the Ilthmarts, who are thinking of another uprising from Lankhmar Below. She is to report back on the readiness of the City of Thieves to defend itself against massive attacks from below. Sheldon will not share this secret with anyone, no matter what happens. Even the most self-serving Lankhmart would try to stop her if her secret mission became known. The only other person in the City of Sevenscore Thousand Smokes who knows Sheldon's hidden purpose is Jendar the Ilthmart, and he won't be telling anyone else.

Unless something prevents her return to Ilthmar, Sheldon will report that Lankhmar is not well prepared for an attack from below, and is only marginally prepared to resist a direct assault.

Adventure Hooks

Sheldon needs to be protected from those who wish her ill. It can be the job of the party to keep her safe. A fee of three rilks per member per week will be paid at the start of each week, with the promise of a bonus at the end of the job.

As for who her real enemies are in Lankhmar, the answer is nearly everyone. Three groups demand special attention:

- The Red Lanterns have hired the Assassins' Brotherhood to kill Sheldon after discovering why she is really here.
- The Vermin Catchers want to know what she's up to, although they don't wish her dead. They have sent a couple of thugs to threaten her and rough her up to find out her intentions.
- The Rat God priests have come to see her twice already, but were not allowed into her room. Unaccustomed to rebuke by those they consider their servants, the priests are becoming more insistent that she conclude her business with them soon.

It is Sheldon's intention to remain in Lankhmar for another five days before she goes to the Rat God's temple to deal with the priests. She is planning to leave the city immediately after visiting the temple.

Experience points for this job will depend on how well the party keeps others away from Sheldon. The promised bonus will not happen, as Sheldon will leave town without paying it. If the PCs try to stop her, she will tell them they only worked five days for a week's pay, so they got two day's pay as a bonus. She will give them each an extra two rilks if pressed, but will also promise never to use them as guards again.

Due to the multiple challenges in this adventure, characters of 5th level or greater are recommended.

Whyseso the Minstrel

Plaza District

Lankhmar is a city of parties and celebration, and parties need entertainment. So, dancers, singers, storytellers, and musicians are needed everywhere in the city.

Whyseso is not a party musician, though he will perform privately for his very good friends on special occasions. He prefers to wander the streets, especially in the Plaza and Festival Districts, playing for anyone who cares to listen. He seldom stays long on any street corner, but spends his day roaming around, looking for a crowd who might pay well for a half hour or so.

Whyseso has an olive complexion and his features suggest an origin in the lands to the far east of Lankhmar. He is very athletic, and his large six foot three inch stature turns more than a few heads wherever he goes. His hair is black and his eyes are brown. He is in his early twenties, but, like most Lankhmarts, he doesn't know exactly how old he is.

After dark, Whyseso likes to party. He has an apartment on Cash Street, but he uses it mainly to store his clothes, of which there are many. Whyseso normally sleeps wherever he is after the final party of the evening winds down.

He fancies himself a ladies' man, and from the attention they give him, his assessment is accurate. Where other men might use this to their advantage, Whyseso is the perfect gentleman at all times. He has such a reputation for impeccable behavior that even the most jealous husband has no fear if his wife flirts with the minstrel. However, Whyseso is far from a model of virtue. He is a paragon of discretion. He does not talk of any of his liaisons, even if a lady chooses not to continue an affair.

Apart from his musical abilities, Whyseso has another, far more secret side to his nature. He is a master thief who targets only the most wealthy and most dangerous targets in Lankhmar. By carefully planning, the wealthiest places in Lankhmar are where Whyseso attends parties and gatherings; the most dangerous places are in the areas he frequents as a minstrel.

In the three years that Whyseso has been actively playing cat burglar in Lankhmar, the Thieves' Guild has never discovered that every target hit by the mystery freelance thief was recently visited by the minstrel in either a professional or social capacity. As with many other unexplained phenomena, the guild blames Midnight for the thefts.

Unfortunately for Whyseso, Midnight made the connection quite quickly, and she wants him in her band of thieves. She has not yet approached him, but she is sure that he will join her or his exploits might reach the ears of the Thieves' Guild's leaders. She may even stoop as far as starting a rumor that Whyseso is really Midnight, just to see how gullible the guild is.

Adventure Hooks

To get an idea of Whyseso's attitude to her band, Midnight wants someone else to "feel him out" before she meets him. Whether taking the job for money, repaying a favor, or getting Midnight into their debt, the PCs should be the agents to make this initial contact with Whyseso.

Reluctant at first, he will ultimately agree to meet Midnight at a time and place of her choosing to discuss the terms of his joining her band. It is up to Midnight whether the PCs, or anyone else, are present at that meeting. Even if it is a private meeting, Midnight will want to guard against interruption, either deliberate or accidental. If she trusts the PCs enough, they could be the guards for that meeting.

The rewards in experience points or social level terms for this job are up to the DM, and should be based on planning and roleplaying techniques.

CHAPTER 4

Places of Interest in Lankhmar

Bolzar's Tannery

Plaza District

In Lankhmar, as in any medieval city, tanned hides are needed for a good many things, including clothing, shelter, and even armor. There are only a few tanneries in Lankhmar, and Bolzar's is the only one which backs against the outer wall.

When it was built, Bolzar said he wanted it near the wall so the stench from the curing hides could blow over the Great Marsh rather than overpowering the neighbors. Nobody really believed he was concerned for his fellow citizens, but nobody cared either. As long as the stench wasn't in their homes, they didn't care about the reasons.

The tannery is really two separate buildings along the wall on Barter Street near Damp Street. The smaller building is where Bolzar lives and stores his hides. He shares the house with his sister, Ruletta, who keeps house and handles most of the sales of tanned and cured hides. The house has only four rooms: a bedroom each for Bolzar and Ruletta, a kitchen and dining area, and the final room of the house is packed with hides. Both Bolzar and Ruletta have been in this business long enough to ignore the odors from the uncured hides. Visitors to their residence are often overwhelmed by the smell during the first few visits.

The large building is the tannery itself. Bolzar spends most of his waking hours here, tending the hides. Its interior is similar to a big barn, with a high roof and a loft along each side where the tanning supplies are stored. The workbench is just inside the front door, so Bolzar can watch who comes and goes to the house, and he can see folk coming to the tannery in time to greet them as they enter. This vantage point also lets him keep an eye out for thieves who might normally come in and steal hides while he was working in the back of the shed.

Bolzar is a solid man, about five feet eight inches in height, and he wieghs 200 pounds. He is well muscled, but his hands are soft and not callused at all. One of the advantages of working with hides is that the natural oils secrete onto the handler's skin, keeping it soft despite the hard work.

Ruletta is a plain-looking woman with a sparkling personality. She has a winning smile and a twinkle in her eyes that soon wins people over despite her appearance. She is also a sharp businesswoman who knows the value of a good hide and knows how to haggle, always stopping just short of a buyer's highest price. She doesn't buy the raw hides, since the abattoir where most of them come from won't do business with her. The owner claims she has no place in a charnel house because she is a woman, but most folk know Ruletta is banned from here because he can get a better price out of Bolzar, whose business sense doesn't equal his skill with the hides.

Bolzar and Ruletta have been in the tannery for twelve years now and they work quite hard. Most of the hides come from domestic animals killed for food. The rest are from wild creatures which are mainly hunted for their pelts. The quality varies greatly in wild animal hides, depending on how well fed the animal was before it was killed and on how it was killed. Poison is the only way to get a hide completely undamaged. Most hides have at least one hole from an arrow or spear.

Bolzar makes light leather armor in the tannery by boiling the cured hides in oil and allowing them to harden. While not as good as that made by an armorer, it isn't anywhere near as expensive either and it is good enough for most people's needs.

The Tanners' Guild suspects Bolzar is buying rare hides on the black market, since he has many more items to sell than he should be able to make from the hides he buys from them. This is not acceptable behavior as the guild charges only a minimal premium on their cost price on the wild animal hides, but they do not appreciate or tolerate competition. The Tanners also suspect Bolzar has a secret exit at the back of his premises and through the outer wall. If this rumor is true, this poses a threat to every person in Lankhmar should someone attack the city and know about the undefended way inside the walls.

Adventure Hooks

- The PCs have returned from an adventure in the wilderness, or even the Great Marsh. Among the things they've brought back are some wild animal hides. Bolzar might buy them for a suitable fee if he can be convinced it isn't a set-up by the Tanners' Guild.

- The rumors about a secret exit through the wall behind Bolzar's tannery are gaining momentum. The Overlord wants the matter investigated quietly. If the rumors are true, he doesn't want to give an enemy any advantage. Despite their many supporters, the rumors are not true. Bolzar is a bit of a shady customer, but he is not stupid. He knows why the walls are there and sleeps better for their defense. To deliberately breach the wall from inside is something he would never contemplate. He will cooperate with any investigation.

- The Tanners want to test the idea that Bolzar is buying pelts from the black market. They need a company of adventurers who will be supplied with a number of very rare hides in excellent condition to offer to Bolzar. Payment for this sting operation is 2 rilks per person and the job should take no more than one day.

  Bolzar will know immediately that this is a setup. The PCs have no pelts from more common animals, and all the pelts are also near perfect. Bolzar has been a tanner long enough to know that no hunter or group of hunters is that good. He will refer the adventurers to the Tanners' Guild, as any upstanding guild member should.

- The Rat God priests of Ilthmar have heard rumors of a secret and unprotected way through the walls of Lankhmar. They will pay handsomely for information about the entrance. This is an open offer to anyone who can give them a lead in planning an attack on the city. They will also vow revenge on any who give them false leads.

The Buttered Loaf

Tenderloin District

Man cannot live by bread alone, and that is why cake was invented. In Lankhmar, as in cities and towns on any world where humans dwell, the bakery is an essential ingredient for life. Some of Lankhmar's bakeries are simple affairs that cater only to the basic needs of bread and rolls. Others are far more elaborate operations capable of cooking the sweetbreads and pastries for a royal banquet. Most of Lankhmar's bakeries rank somewhere in between the two extremes.

The Buttered Loaf is one of these "in-between" bakeries. It is located on the south side of Rats Alley in the Tenderloin District. It is close to the Temple District, but gains the lower rent from a lower social area.

Bjorn the baker is the owner of the Buttered Loaf, but he does not own the building. He is a stout gentleman of some forty summers, just over five feet six inches tall and larger than that around his middle. He has a ruddy complexion caused by his constant work near the ovens, his weight, and his constant companion—a bottle of cheap wine.

Bjorn is mostly cheerful, but by mid-afternoon, his cheer begins to wane until, in the early evening, he is utterly obnoxious. This change is mostly due to his work times, since he lights his ovens before dawn, and he has been up kneading the bread for at least an hour before this.

Bjorn and his wife Neeva have been running the bakery for two years now, and they have built up a solid regular clientele. Neeva is a slim woman with wavy brown hair and a ready smile. They have no children, but Neeva often gives the local street kids leftover cakes and bread from the shop around closing time. This effectively recruits young volunteer watchmen for the bakery, as the kids want to continue getting free food. Taking turns at watching the bakery is a small price to pay for guaranteed meals, and Neeva and Bjorn are happy since feeding the leftovers to the street kids costs less than hiring guards.

Recently, there has been a spate of robberies around the bakery and the Buttered Loaf has not escaped the thieves' attention. Bjorn is very angry about this and has been to see the area boss of the Thieves' Guild to complain. He pays his "insurance" every month, and believes he is entitled to the protection he is paying for.

The local boss agrees with Bjorn. It is much less effort for a thief to sell insurance than it is to plan and execute a successful heist. But, the insurance has to be effective and mean something, or people will stop paying it. The problem is not the Thieves' Guild or the street kids, who are feeling quite miserable about letting someone slip through unnoticed. The Thieves' Guild is blaming Midnight's band, as they do for virtually everything that goes wrong these days. Most of the recent break-ins have netted the thief little of value, including what was stolen at the Buttered Loaf. It just doesn't seem to fit Midnight's requirements of a high class place with high value items the owner can afford to lose.

Neeva has suggested to Bjorn that they move to a tenement for a while, instead of their upstairs apartment, but Bjorn won't hear of it. He insists no harm will come to them, and that the thief will not return, having gotten very little the first time. The only concession Bjorn has made for their safety is to hide the money each night.

For now, it is business as usual. Fresh loaves are ready just after dawn each morning, and cost five agols each. Fancy breads, such as stickbread, or twisted loaves, cost eight agols each. Bread with poppy seeds on top, or mixed grain through the loaf, cost ten agols each. The shop also has a selection of sweetbreads, mostly fruit danishes. Small danishes cost seven agols and large ones cost 15 agols. Bjorn bakes only five or six dozen danishes each day and they sell out by around midday.

Adventure Hooks

Since the first robbery, Bjorn has been on the lookout for anyone suspicious. He hasn't spotted anyone, but the Buttered Loaf is broken into again one night (along with three other nearby buildings). The street kids once again saw nothing.

The residents in the area are getting edgy about the increase in break-ins. Few believe the stories about Midnight being responsible and they are very wise. It just isn't her style, although she is aware that her group is being blamed for them. She has an interest in finding out who is committing these crimes against ordinary citizens in her name.

Bjorn also wants to know who's responsible for the break-ins, especially the two incidents at his bakery. He plans to bake the offender slowly in his ovens.

The PCs can be sent by Midnight to investigate, or they can be regular customers and friends of Bjorn eager to help him out. They might also be hired by Bjorn and his neighbors to solve the mystery.

A new gang has moved into the city and it wants to take over this part of the city, though they don't want a war with the Thieves' Guild over who owns the streets. To their line of thinking, if they scare the current residents and merchants out of the area, they can take over the empty buildings and rent them to new tenants with no long standing payoffs to the Thieves' Guild. They haven't been spotted by the kids because they come up through manholes behind the buildings, in dead end alleys where the kids don't normally watch for intruders.

What this new group has not taken into account is that even gangs pay protection to the Thieves' Guild, or they get shut down. If their plans are even remotely successful, they will learn this very quickly.

If the party discovers the plot, they should tell either Midnight or the Thieves' Guild and let them handle it. The gang is too big for any adventuring company to handle alone. The rewards for this adventure should be mostly fame and social levels, as money will be minimal.

Calvin's Apothecary

Tenderloin District

Calvin the Apothecary lives near where the Tenderloin and Cash Districts meet. While apothecaries are not uncommon in Lankhmar, Calvin is a unique member of his profession. He is a member of the Order of Apothecaries, but he pays no dues. He has been in business in the same shop for as long as anyone can remember, and he never seems to get any older. He prepares potions and poultices that other members of the order have never heard of. There is no known ailment that he cannot provide a treatment for, no pain he cannot lessen with one of his many salves or potions. None of his medicines detect as magical, since all are natural substances with no arcane enhancements.

Calvin appears to be about 40 years old. He is a heavy-set man, standing about five feet eleven inches tall, with a pot belly and balding pate. Despite his paunch, his broad shoulders suggest a powerful build more akin to a far more active lifestyle. Calvin always spends his days in his shop, so it is a mystery how he got his physique. Most folk who think about it say he looks more like a blacksmith than an apothecary.

It is also known that he must be much older than 40, but the Lankhmart calendar is notoriously inaccurate and proving a person's age is nigh impossible. Calvin admits to being 43, and has been admitting to that age for as long as anyone can remember. In truth, Calvin is over 100 years old. He discovered the means of making *potions of longevity*, but he has kept that a strict secret. He puts his good health down to a healthy lifestyle and regular exercise, which he seldom seems to get.

Calvin's shop is filled with many interesting odors. There are bunches of dried herbs hanging from the ceiling, all manner of liquids in glass an earthen jugs, and various animal parts in small cabinets. His preparation room is at the back of the shop, behind a heavy curtain. While working back in the preparation room, he can keep an ear out for customers while keeping his methods and recipes secret.

He lives above the shop in a simple but comfortable apartment. The other apartment on the second floor is empty, and so are both apartments on the third floor. Calvin is happy to rent them out, but few can stand the smells from the shop that permeate the rooms and everything in them.

Virtually all freelancers use Calvin's shop for their healing salves and poison antidotes. Most apothecaries sell only to guilds, and members must buy through them, but Calvin was a freelancer himself many years ago, and also has a soft spot for adventurers. His prices are often set depending on how well off a customer is, or appears to be. Regular customers in a pinch can get credit, and Calvin doesn't keep very good books. Guilds and nobles always pay full price for any medicines they purchase. The Thieves' Guild is an exception, and it gets a discount on purchases in lieu of the normal protection money they collect from other businesses.

Adventure Hooks

There are no specific adventures in or around Calvin's shop. Nonguild adventurers are almost certain to be customers, and guild members are probably customers indirectly. A chance encounter with some ruffians who are new in town and try to establish themselves by strong-arming Calvin could lead to a grudge war between the PCs and the ruffians.

Alternatively, if the PCs are new in town, they may desperately need Calvin's help for a wounded or dying companion, and have no means of paying for it. Calvin could send them into the Great Marsh to find some rare fungus he needs in exchange for helping their friend.

The one thing Calvin will never sell or give away is a *potion of longevity*. These secret magical potions are for his use alone.

Social levels and experience are not the issue here. Just as you do in real life, your characters should do some things for no reward other than the lesson learned or the feeling of having helped a friend.

The Cat O' Nines

Tenderloin District

The City of Sevenscore Thousand Smokes is home to many houses of ill repute, bordellos, and brothels. Among the more infamous of these is the Cat O' Nines, a large establishment on the corner of Craft and Carter Streets. There are six floors above ground and at least two below ground. The entrance to the building is in a lane off Craft Street. The reception area consists of several comfortable lounges, a reception desk, and two small booths where clients may view drawings of the services offered here. The other five upper floors are split in half. The left half (as viewed from the entrance) holds the private quarters of the staff and is off-limits to anyone who does not work at the Cat O' Nines. Even visits from friends and relatives are banned, as the staff members need their privacy and rest when they are not working. This half of the building is reached from a staircase that goes from the reception area, behind the desk, all the way to the top with landings on each floor. There is no access to the private quarters from any of the upper floor work areas.

The larger half of each floor contains several workrooms. The tastes of any client may be satisfied in these rooms, each of which is specially suited to a particular task. It is the nature of these tasks that sends shudders through even the most twisted Lankhmart. Rumors are rife about the unsavory activity taking place here.

As sick and twisted as the upper floors can be, the underground floors are believed to be worse yet. For exorbitant fees, clients may witness an arena show of horrific activities deemed illegal even in Lankhmar. The authorities cannot shut the place down without proof of such operations and that proof has never been obtained. All searches of the basements have found no evidence save dust, bric-a-brac, and a few animal cages. Guards' attempts to buy seats at one of these shows have met with denial that such things exist, proving the receptionists are either well trained about these matters or the stories have no apparent basis in fact.

The owners of the Cat O' Nines are the workers and they each pay their dues to the House of the Red Lanterns. They also pay protection money to the Thieves' Guild and the Slayers' Brotherhood (as well as the city guard and the Overlord himself, if the stories are to be believed). A very long time ago, a journeyman thief broke into the Cat O' Nines to see what he could steal. His body was discovered three days later in an alleyway near the docks, naked and mutilated. No member of the Thieves' Guild has attempted to steal from the Cat since.

Each of the 25 to 30 workers takes a turn at the reception desk. This duty occurs every ten days or so, and each worker must spend six hours greeting the customers, finding out what services they want, and collecting their fees. All staff persons are scrupulous in their accounting of fees collected on their shift. Twice in the past, workers have attempted to skim a little off the top for themselves. Twice they were caught and their corpses were found in the River Hlal. The last occurrence was five years ago.

New staff are taken on only when the demand is high, but once a worker is in, he or she can stay as long as desired. The house cannot accommodate more than 30 persons in the private quarters, so this is the upper limit on staff. The lower limit is variable, but if it falls below 25, the staff often cannot meet all the demands of their clients.

About two-thirds of the workers at the Cat O' Nines are female. Only half the male staff persons are available to clients, since the other males act as bouncers if necessary, and set up rooms to clients' specifications. These staff persons are paid a monthly salary of 50 gold rilks in addition to their keep.

At the end of each month, the fees and protection money are paid out, and the remaining funds are distributed among the staff according to how much money they brought in that month. The standard take per staff person is 250 rilks per month, though some who indulge the more bizarre customers can make up to 1000 rilks.

Fees vary considerably, from a single smerduk to several hundred rilks. There is no specific fee for services, though the receptionist tries to get the maximum payment possible for each service, depending mainly on the client's apparent wealth. Access to the lower rooms is restricted to those who are known to the staff, and who have been thoroughly checked out to ensure they will not report what they see there. New customers to the lower levels are required to be introduced by a known client.

The more genteel folk of Lankhmar have tried several times to have the Cat O' Nines closed down. It is too twisted and depraved, even by the lax standards here. The city guards want it closed too, but they have no legal reason to step in. Even the House of the Red Lanterns wants the place closed, but they can do nothing overt, as all the workers are guild members. The income from the Cat is considerable for the Red Lanterns, the city guard, and the Thieves and Slayers alike. All of them are well aware that, while closing the place down would be good for everyone in general terms, it would be bad for their coffers and this is probably the main reason the Cat O' Nines is still operating.

Ideally, a freelance outfit of do-gooders could close it down, then the Slayers would deal with the freelancers as punishment for loss of income. After a short time, the Red Lanterns could reopen the Cat with a more socially acceptable range of services. The Thieves and the city guards are still unsure if they are willing to forego so much money, so nothing has been arranged yet.

Adventure Hooks

Just about everyone in Lankhmar wants the Cat O' Nines out of business, but nobody wants to be known as the active party in closing them down. It's in everyone's fiscal interests for the Cat to keep going, but it's just too depraved to be allowed to continue.

A party of non-native Lankhmarts, or even citizens with no connections to the city guards, the Overlord, the House of the Red Lanterns, or any of the nearby residents would be the perfect tool to either get evidence of what happens below ground in the Cat, or to find some other way of closing it down, whether through legal means or something as drastic as burning it down.

Payment for the job would be quite high, as much as 40 rilks per party member. There would be no rise in social level since the party could never claim the "credit" for the deed. To do so would invite retribution from the Slayers' Brotherhood. If the mission is not kept secret, the Red Lanterns would be forced to employ the Slayers to act against those PCs who acted against the guild. The Slayers would be happy to act against the party for free, as they make a tidy sum from the Cat and will miss the income. However, if they can get paid for doing a job, they will take that course rather than be driven by vengeance.

Whoever hires the party to close the Cat down may wish to cover themselves by betraying the party to the Slayers, or publicly denouncing them if the building or any of its occupants are harmed in any way.

For those who want the Cat closed, it's a no-lose situation. They can have it closed down, then ensure that those responsible are punished for depriving so many people of the income they've come to expect from it. If any serious undercover investigation is done, the rumors about the basement levels will be proved true. The evidence is always cleaned up and bodies disposed of, but traces can be found if the searchers are determined.

The End Gate

Plaza District

Perhaps the strangest of all the gates to Lankhmar, the End Gate has no apparent purpose. The Grain Gate is the best way into the city for traders wishing to use the docks; the Grand Gate is the main thoroughfare for travelers; the Marsh Gate leads to the Great Marsh and beyond; but there is no obvious reason for the End Gate to exist.

Lankhmarts being what they are, and the End Gate being conveniently located near the Plaza of Dark Delights, the gate has become the standard way in for those whose business or goods are less than honest, even in a city where honesty is not a prized commodity. Through the End Gate come illicit goods, the possession of which earns a lengthy term in the slave pens if the owners are caught. Kidnapers use this gate to spirit their captives away from the city, and known felons use the End Gate to sneak in and out of the city at any time, day or night.

In a city where corrupt guards are the standard, the guards on the End Gate were legendary in their corruption. Captain Scress and his band of 12 guardsmen were far more comfortable than they had any right to be on their salaries. No matter who or what was to be smuggled into or out of the city, they were always capable of being bribed. The minimum bribe they accepted was one smerduk, while bribes of up to 20 rilks were not uncommon. There were rumors that some merchants without manifests for their goods often preferred to bribe Scress and his men rather than go through the rigors of an audit from the city accountants.

Eventually, even in Lankhmar, a corrupt official will go too far. So it was recently with Captain Scress. A daughter of the noble family Ridoa was kidnapped and held for ransom. To prevent the wealthy family from hiring mercenaries to track down the daughter, the kidnapers took her to Quarmall. They left through the End Gate, paying a bribe of 13 rilks for the guards not to notice their passing.

The ransom was paid by the family, but the kidnapers did not return their hostage since the Quarmalls paid 1,000 rilks for her. The kidnapers did not ask why she was worth so much, nor what the Quarmalls planned to do with her. She will not be coming back, ever.

The Ridoa family was furious. Kidnaping and extortion are a part of life in Lankhmar, but there are certain rules that must be followed, including the return of hostages once the ransom is paid. The Slayers were hired to find the kidnapers, which they did. The Overlord had no choice but to order their executions despite the return of the ransom and the pleas of the Extortionists' Guild for clemency. Before they died, the kidnapers implicated Scress and the guards in the plot, detailing their exact method of egress from the city, and the bribe paid. Scress was disgraced and he and his men were dismissed from their duties, though they were all lucky to not be included in the public executions.

In an attempt to pacify the nobility, a supposedly incorruptible guard captain, Redlock, and his troop of 10 guards was appointed with orders to tighten the screws on illicit entries. What no one in Lankhmar expected was that the new troop of guards really are incorruptible and take their job very seriously. Since their appointment two days ago, they have arrested four merchants attempting to evade the trade tax, caught eight known felons trying to sneak through the gate, and foiled three kidnaping plots.

There are too many guards for anyone to openly attack them, and the Overlord has no valid reason to remove them. After all, they are doing what they were employed to do. Secretly, the Overlord is quite pleased with the guards, but he can't acknowledge that for fear of annoying the thieves, assassins, and extortionists even more.

While most folk in the city agree that the guards have to go, there is no workable plan to remove them as yet. Assassination is not an option, since killing even one guard would bring all the city guards down on the perpetrators, and even the Assassins' Brotherhood could not prevent this.

Bribery has not worked yet on these new guards, although there are those who believe that every man has his price, even Captain Redlock. Thus far, the offers have obviously not been high enough. Redlock has stated that he will arrest anyone attempting to bribe his guards, but most of the men would rather just refuse the bribe than report the matter to Redlock. Bribes are still being offered, but there are rumors that one guard was offered a gluditch to look away, but refused.

Members of the Extortionists' Guild are currently planning an elaborate scheme to frame Redlock for a crime or catch him in some transgression (whether true or staged) and blackmail him. It is widely known that Redlock's wife insists on fidelity and the Extortionists are attempting to maneuver Redlock into compromising positions. If necessary, the guild is prepared to kidnap Redlock and drug him to set up this blackmail scheme.

The guild is still smarting over the Ridoa kidnaping and wants revenge against the authorities. Getting rid of a nuisance guard contingent is an added bonus, and it made the choice of targets easy for the guild.

Adventure Hooks

There are two possibilities for adventure here. The party can be some of the new guards, having all manner of attempts made to corrupt or even kill them. Remember that killing a member of the city guard is likely to get the perpetrator killed, too. Depending on what best fits your campaign, you may want the PC guards to be corrupted or to remain inviolate no matter what. Experience points should be awarded for staying within character alignments in this case. Social levels should only be awarded to guards who stay true to their alignments. Corrupt guards are plentiful in Lankhmar, so perhaps Redlock's guards are acting like this deliberately to get noticed? Once noticed by someone important, they might gain bigger tasks than guarding a city gate. While incorruptible, they are not immune to ambition.

On the other side of the coin, the PCs may be trying to leave Lankhmar with some contraband, or they may currently be wanted felons for some crime, real or imagined. In this case, the challenge is to get past the honest guards and out the End Gate. As the guards have been in place for only two days, the PCs have obviously been in hiding for some reason and have not heard the news. Once they reach the gate, to turn around and try another exit would arouse suspicion, so they will have to continue or risk a chase through the streets. Experience in this case should be awarded based on how well each character plays his part in the escape. Bear in mind that not all party members should necessarily speak with the guards. Keeping a sharp eye out for trouble is always important. Social levels can play a large part in any negotiations, since a high social level means that the character will be recognized and that the guards will be anxious not to offend such an important person without good reason. A low social level should guarantee anonymity, but it can also mean a somewhat rougher time with the guards who are quite happy to offend a nobody. Even honest guards like to throw their weight around just so people know who is in charge in Lankhmar.

The Haunted House

Plaza District

Next to the Bazaar of the Bizarre is an abandoned tenement that has remained unoccupied since the Devourers opened their ill-fated business next door. After all, who wants to live next to a haunted building, no matter how cheap the rent is?

The tenement is four stories of decaying timber and crumbling stone that would be condemned in a modern society. It is so creepy and decrepit that not even the rats will live in it. In its long-ago heyday, the building was used by itinerant market vendors as a close and reasonably priced shelter for excess stock while they hawked their wares in the nearby Plaza.

Recently, there have been stories of lights in the windows, and noises coming from the building late at night. A number of people have disappeared without trace, and the last place anyone can remember seeing any of the missing people is in the Plaza, but nothing more specific than that. Most Lankhmarts put the noises down to falling timbers or plaster, or they dismiss them as stories to frighten young children to sleep. In any case, nobody has seen fit to investigate the building, especially not at night.

This current state of indifference about the Haunted House is exactly how the new inhabitants want it. The ghouls who have moved into the tenement are an advance scouting party, sent to find ways of taking Lankhmar by stealth. The ghouls desperately want the city for themselves, but realize they have neither the numbers nor the resources to take it by force. The disappearing folk are reduced to dinner for the ghouls, although a number of them were killed by other parties (though the ghouls claimed the bodies as food later).

There are 18 ghouls in the tenement at the moment, and they have made contact with Lankhmar Below with a view to enlisting the aid of the rats with their plans. So far, the rats have mostly helped by sneaking the ghouls into the basement of the building, so nobody knows they're here.

The rats are quite interested in helping bring Lankhmar to its knees, as they have a lot of built-up resentment over Vermin Day and welcome the chance to pay back the humans. Also, if the ghouls attack, it doesn't matter to the rats who wins, since the victor will be weakened and unprepared for an invasion from below.

Adventure Hooks

The characters may go into the abandoned building as a dare from a rival band. Status among the various adventuring companies in Lankhmar is often subject to silly challenges brought by one group against another. To refuse a dare, no matter how silly it may be, lowers the company's status in adventurers' circles.

Perhaps the party is going in at the request of some of the Plaza's vendors who are finally taking serious notice of the noises and occasional lights. If so, they should expect to be getting well paid for their troubles, even if they believe there's nothing to find. Alternatively, a family member or friend could have disappeared in the Plaza and the characters are looking for them. It could even be a party member who's gone missing.

Eventually, the PCs will enter the building and, after searching for a while, they will be set upon by the ghouls. If possible, the ghouls will attack anyone who gets separated from the others. The ghouls place more emphasis on stopping the PCs from calling for help than on killing them or knocking them out.

If the party members go to the basement, they will be attacked as soon as the last of them reaches the bottom of the stairs. Once they reveal themselves, the ghouls will try to prevent anyone escaping, even at the cost of some of their lives. The ghouls are AC 7 due to the low light, have 18 hit points each, and a THAC0 of 17. Each is worth 175 XP.

Whatever reason the PCs had for entering, they will be hailed as heroes of Lankhmar if they succeed. They will each gain at least three social levels and will have bronze busts placed in the Plaza on pedestals. They may even get an official reception in their honor.

Iscar's

Tenderloin District

Moneylenders in Lankhmar are simply fences with a better title. Famous among the fences of old was Iscar. No item was too hot or too hard to handle for Iscar. He paid top rates and charged outrageous prices, but he got away with it for many years. Eventually, he fenced some art that had been stolen from the Overlord, and he was publicly executed for his folly.

Even after death, Iscar still has an influence in the stolen goods market. He had four assistants who all escaped the hangman's noose and now run the moneylender's shop in Iscar's name.

Iscar's is a five-story building on Cash Street in the Tenderloin District. The ground floor is where the common goods for sale are displayed. It is also where all those desiring a "loan" do their business in private rooms.

The second floor is occupied by Marko, the gem and jewelry expert. He appraises all the items in his area here. He also controls the hotter items that can't be displayed downstairs. Marko is a roly-poly man, standing five feet tall and weighing in at over 200 pounds. He is very quiet and studious, and is an expert in gemology and whitesmithing. Marko is 28 years old, and has dark brown eyes. He is bald, with only a tuft of hair just behind each ear.

The third floor is the domain of Cosap, the fine-arts fence. Cosap is a lithe woman about 25 years old with striking, angular features that would never be called pretty. She is five feet three inches tall, and she has dark hair and green eyes. Cosap is knowledgeable about objets d'art, but is not yet an expert. So, Iscar's sometimes lets valuable artwork go for much lower prices than they could have fetched. The owners don't know they've done it, so there are no retaliations against Cosap. She sometimes realizes too late what she has done and makes a mental note to be more careful next time. As she is quite intelligent, Cosap never makes the same mistake twice. Given time, she will become one of Lankhmar's most qualified art appraisers and dealers.

The fourth floor is inhabited by Jarrus. The oldest of the group at 34, he is the unofficial leader. It's not a major function as each of the four has their own specialty and the others defer to the expert in most cases. Jarrus is five feet seven inches tall, and is heavily built. He drinks too much, and has a sizeable paunch on his once-powerful frame. His expertise is in items from eastern lands, like rugs, statues, jade, and exotic spices.

The top floor is the domain of Ardaman. It has barred windows and a locked door at the top of the stairs. Only Ardaman and Jarrus have keys to the door. In Ardaman's rooms are unusual weapons, and those of fine workmanship. They are not on display on the ground floor as the temptation to steal them would be too great for many thieves. Those wanting to examine weapons need only ask and Ardaman will bring down an appropriate selection for viewing. The other area that Ardaman looks after is magic. Any items of magic that are traded through Iscar's are handled by Ardaman. He pays only a fraction of their value and sells them for as much as he can get. Some magical items are never sold, but are kept by the moneylenders for their own use. They are rumored to have six or seven items of a protective nature each, though just what each of them has is a closely guarded secret.

Ardaman is not a wizard, but is more like a sage. He is five feet nine inches tall, and has snow-white hair, despite his 27 years. He walks with a limp and stoops a lot, the result of being run down by a wagon when he was a child. He suffers a lot from his injuries, but tries hard to keep a brave face on things. He is quite friendly to those who get to know him and will share his knowledge of magic (but not its worth) willingly with anyone he trusts enough to call a friend.

The four occupants work well together to ensure a good income for the business. There has never been a rumor of any of them trying to cheat the others, nor even a hint of any impropriety. That is a legacy from Iscar to his successors, and it shows there is, strangely enough, honor among thieves.

Adventure Hooks

- All Lankhmart moneylenders need a guard force from time to time, unless they have permanent guards. Unemployed adventuring companies are normally cheaper to hire than squads from the Slayers' Brotherhood or the Mercenaries' guild.
- Stolen goods which are too hot to keep need to be fenced quickly, for whatever the thief can get. Iscar's fences pay on the spot and don't ask questions about the origin of items. This makes it ideal for adventuring thieves who find more than they plan for in a raid, or who are spotted by and are on the run from the guards.
- Just because an item is not available for sale on the ground floor doesn't mean Iscar's doesn't have one. A desperate adventurer or adventuring band may want to raid the shop and see for themselves what is available. If they are caught, Jarrus and the others will deal with them very harshly (and possibly permanently).
- Anyone who has had a valuable or unusual item stolen knows that Iscar's is a good place to start looking. If they can't prove ownership of an item, they often have to buy the item back. As proving ownership is difficult and items tend to be sold before legal matters are resolved, some folk try to steal their goods back. The clever ones steal from the eventual purchaser, not the shop.

The Saltmarsh Inn

Tenderloin District

Among the many inns and taverns in the City of Sevenscore Thousand Smokes, the Saltmarsh Inn is one of the most decrepit. It is neither fashionable nor fancy, and it does not attract the reverse snobbery clientele like other establishments. The building is as old and tired as it looks, and it should have been torn down many years ago.

The inn is up by the Temple District, on Carter Street. It is only three stories tall with a small cellar. The whole ground floor is the bar and kitchen, and the top two floors each contain eight rooms for rent.

The owner, Tolara, is an imposing woman who will hear no wrong said of her inn. She is almost as wide as she is tall, and there are few in the Tenderloin District who willingly cross her. For all her bulk and temper, Tolara is a kindly soul. She takes in people who are down on their luck and gives them a meal and a bed for up to two nights; in exchange, she has them do some minor work at the inn. Very occasionally she will take in an unemployed tradesman, and this is the only way the inn gets any of the repair work it does need.

Tolara keeps the inn clean on the inside, and the rooms are quite reasonably priced, one agol per night. The ale is always good and plentiful, and meals are tasty, nutritious, and inexpensive.

Bad or rowdy behavior is not tolerated in the Saltmarsh, and offenders are removed by either Tolara or one of her regular customers. For all its outward appearance, the Saltmarsh is a place where an entire family can go for a meal or to celebrate a birthday or other occasion.

There are many rumors about why the Saltmarsh hasn't been demolished. The one given the most credence is that the Thieves' Guild officers are the real owners, using Tolara as a front, and they use the inn as a meeting place and as a place to stash stolen property that is too hot to fence for a while. There are also stories that it may be one of the Thieves' Guild's secret ways into Lankhmar Below. None of the stories has been proven (or disproved).

Apart from Tolara, the other notable person found regularly in the Saltmarsh Inn is Grufet the gambler. He is an unshaven man, well over six feet tall and as thin as a rake. He will play any sort of gambling game with anyone, and he loses just often enough to not be accused of cheating. Grufet doesn't have to cheat, since he is quite good at the shell game and at knucklebones. Sometimes, he will throw a game just so folk don't think he's found a way to cheat.

Grufet's favorite game of all is Loser, a game played with a deck of special cards of five colors and numbered one to eight in each color. The object of the game is to play all your cards before anyone else does. Two, three, or four can play. Each player is dealt seven cards and a card is turned face up. To play a card, the player must match either the color or the number of the current face up card. If a player cannot play a card, they must draw from the deck. If the deck is exhausted, the top face-up card is removed and the rest are shuffled and again placed face down to continue the game. When one player has played all his cards, the others pay according to the value of the cards they have left. All red cards are face value (one to 10); blue are reverse value cards (in other words, the 1 is worth 10 points and the 10 worth one point); black cards are worth double their face value; green cards triple the value on their faces; and yellow cards reduce the debt by their face value, but never below zero. The amount of the bet is agreed before the game, but one to five tiks per point is normal. Grufet cheats at this game a lot, by rigging the deal on his turn. He also sometimes plays two cards instead of one. In spite of his cheating, and his skill at Loser, he sometimes loses a little money by throwing a game just so his opponents don't get suspicious. Tolara knows what he is up to, but the gamblers buy a lot of food and drink, so she says nothing.

Adventure Hooks

- The rumors about the Thieves' Guild owning the Saltmarsh are untrue, and can be checked out if anyone really wants to know.

- The rumors about secret access to Lankhmar Below are true, and Tolara will show the tunnels to anyone she trusts who promises not to make war on the rats. Whatever else they do below, Tolara doesn't care and doesn't want to know. The inn is fairly close to the Ferret Hole if anyone felt inclined to sneak in from below and clean it out. This is not an option recommended for PCs below 12th level.

- If the PCs are short of money and fancy their chances, they could challenge Grufet to a game of Loser. If they lose and don't pay, Grufet will send the Slayers after them. If they win, Grufet will pay, then send the Slayers after them.

- Grufet has finally been caught cheating, by the PCs, and needs to be taught a lesson. The best lesson would be to beat him at his own game and relieve him of some money, then let him know he was spotted and cheated back as punishment.

- Rat God worshippers may wish to search through the secret tunnels. What can be used to get into Lankhmar Below can be used to get out as well. The PCs can either be the searchers (if they worship the Rat God), or be customers (either chance or regular) in the inn when the rats burst out of the cellar. There are 28 rats, each with 14 hit points. Their THAC0 is 17, their AC is 7, and they bite for 1-6 points plus the possibility of disease. Each is worth 92 XP. There are two wererats with them, each with 19 hit points. They can attack with their swords for 1-8 damage, or bite for 1-6 plus the possibility of disease. Their THAC0 is 16 and each is worth 186 XP. The wererats are affected only by silver or magical weapons.

The Squeaky Stoop

Tenderloin District

The City of Sevenscore Thousand Smokes does not have that many brothels, but sometimes it seems that way. Among the better-known bordellos is the Squeaky Stoop, a clean and well-kept establishment in the Tenderloin District.

The proprietor, Madam Durgal, is particular about the type of people she will allow to work for her, and she screens her customers just as carefully. The result is a brothel with a reputation for good service and integrity, and, of course, total confidentiality. Some of Lankhmar's leading lights have frequented the Squeaky Stoop, but no one in the house talks about who their clients are to outsiders.

The brothel takes the top three floors of a five-story tenement, the bottom two floors being rented apartments. Madam Durgal owns the whole building, and her tenants know better than to take an interest in who comes and goes on the upper floors. There are separate entrances for the brothel and the apartments, and several concealed exits to permit clients to leave unobtrusively. Regular clients are told how to open these doorways from the outside so they can get in as unnoticed as they get out.

There are fifteen girls working at the Squeaky Stoop and new girls are taken on as others leave or retire. It is not uncommon for a client to marry a favorite girl, or to run off with her to another part of Nehwon. The only rule Madam Durgal insists on is that the girls never reveal the identities of their clients to anyone.

As a safeguard, most clients use assumed names and aliases, but anyone whose social level is 10 or higher is likely to be recognized regardless of what name is used. Naturally, it is those clients whose social levels are highest who most wish to avoid being linked with a brothel, even one with a good reputation.

In the past few weeks, as tenants have moved on, Madam Durgal has not taken in new ones. The building is getting run down and she intends to close the building for a few weeks while maintenance is done on it. The external maintenance work also gives her an opportunity to do a facelift of the brothel, with new paint, new furniture, new curtains, and other remodeling.

While the refurbishment will be expensive, it is not the cost that most worries Madam Durgal. The stripping and replacement of rotted timbers will necessarily expose some of the hidden passages behind the walls, and may risk revealing the secret ways in and out of the Stoop. Such revelations could do immense damage to her business, and Madam Durgal is willing to go to great lengths to prevent any secrets getting out.

Many wives in Lankhmar suspect their husbands visit the Squeaky Stoop from time to time. Some of their suspicions are true, although most are not. Only those men with impeccable backgrounds are accepted as clients.

Still, to find out what their husbands are (or are not) up to behind their backs, the wives must investigate, or have someone investigate for them. The concept of private detectives does not exist in Lankhmar, but there are those in the Thieves' Guild who will spy on others for a fee. If they know in advance what answer the client wants, they will usually make sure that's the answer they come up with, or go to the person being investigated and demand even more money not to reveal what's going on even if that is nothing. Truth is not important to these folk, but if, in the course of an investigation, they found one of the hidden entrances to the Squeaky Stoop, careful surveillance over a week or two could produce enough evidence to blackmail one or more of Madam Durgal's clients.

If even one client were linked to the Stoop, its reputation would be ruined. False accusations have been made in the past, and will be made again in the future, but these are easily and quickly disproved if people are willing to listen.

Adventure Hooks

In order to keep her secrets safe, Madam Durgal needs to hire several trustworthy people to keep an eye on the workmen doing the refurbishment and also to watch for passersby who show too much interest in the building alterations. Only a party with high social levels and impeccable reputations will be hired for this job.

The building work will take three weeks according to the foreman, but the job will inevitably be delayed by weather or lack of materials (or other suitable excuses to stretch out the job by an additional week or two). The actual time to finish the job will be at least four weeks and may be up to six if the DM wishes to keep the party busy.

Madam Durgal is paying three rilks per person per week, but she expects a 24-hour watch to be kept over the place for her money. The PCs can stay in the ground floor apartments if they wish, moving around as the workmen need access to each apartment.

During the building, two of the workmen will show too much interest in the hidden passageways. They are both working for nobles' wives who suspect their husbands of cheating. Both are wrong, at least as far as patronizing the Squeaky Stoop.

At least once each week, someone will linger too long across the street. It could be a curious thief, an irate wife, or just an innocent passerby looking at the building. None of these encounters lead to anything, but the people need to be moved on before they see something they should not.

When the job is completed, the builders and PCs will be paid a bonus 10 rilks each to ensure their silence over anything they may have seen while they were working at the Squeaky Stoop. If anyone in the party uses any information gained for their own ends, such actions should be very damaging to their reputations and social level. Even in Lankhmar, there must be some honor in any contract undertaken.

The Twin Taverns

Plaza District

In the Plaza District, on Festival Street, are two taverns immediately opposite each other. The Wooden Leg and the Rising Moon are quite different in appearance and get their collective name of the Twin Taverns since they are owned and run by twin brothers, Hamol and Tamol.

Hamol is the owner of the Wooden Leg, which he took as payment for some debts when he was a moneylender. Tamol owns the Rising Moon and has owned it as long as any of the regulars can remember.

The Wooden Leg

The Wooden Leg is five stories tall, the first two of which are taprooms. There is a huge cellar under the tavern to store enough liquor and ale to keep both taverns stocked. Hamol has a permanent guard from the Slayers' Brotherhood on site to protect the valuable stock in the cellar and to remind patrons that unseemly behavior will be dealt with swiftly and, if necessary, permanently.

The upper three floors contain rooms that can be rented by the hour, the day, or the week. Several adventuring companies use rooms on the upper floors as offices and rendezvous points for prospective employers. These companies pay a special rate of two weeks rent per month, and their rooms are often let overnight to itinerant patrons. Hamol always removes any personal property to the cellar if he intends to let the room overnight.

Hamol himself is a large man, broad in the shoulders and barrel-chested, but he is getting fat. He stands a little under six feet tall and that, combined with his flaming red hair and temper to match, keeps many patrons in line when he is around. He is deceptively quick for such a bulky person, and he can grab a man's wrist before a knife or a sword can be drawn. Hamol has been known to break peoples' wrists if they don't release their weapon hilts quickly enough.

The ale in the ground floor taproom costs two agols per pitcher, mead costs one agol per flagon, and watered wine costs five agols per flagon. Food is provided at one rilk for all you can eat. The fare normally consists of a vegetable stew with a little meat, fresh bread, cheese, and soup. It's simple fare, but nutritious, and Hamol makes a tidy profit on food sales.

The second floor bar charges half as much again as downstairs, and does not serve food at all. It's main draw is the table service, and the discreet booths used by patrons to arrange contracts, both legal and illegal.

The Rising Moon

The Rising Moon is only four stories tall and boasts only one taproom, albeit a large one. The prices in the Rising Moon are the same as the ground floor taproom in the Wooden Leg, except for the food. Tamol charges three smerduks for his smorgasbord, but always has hearty stews of chicken, beef, and mutton in addition to the other fare.

The upper floors of the Rising Moon are available for rent. Tamol charges one rilk per room per night. If the room is needed for less than a night, the fee is still one rilk. If six or seven people want to cram into one room to sleep, it's still one rilk. If an adventuring company wants to rent a room on a permanent basis, the fee is one rilk per night, payable one week in advance. Tamol has had experience with adventuring companies going out "for a few days" and coming back several weeks later, or not coming back at all.

Unlike his brother, Tamol will not let a room twice. He charges more than Hamol, but he guarantees security to his tenants. This guarantee not only includes not reletting the room, but also uninterrupted nights. Tamol has two bouncers on duty around the clock to keep the peace. There are eight bouncers all together, and those who are not on duty are either sleeping upstairs or working behind the bar or in the cellar. Each bouncer is a 5th-level fighter armed with two daggers and wearing a chain mail shirt under his jerkin. They each have 41 hit points and get bonuses of +2 to attack and +3 to damage due to their exceptional Strength scores. The bouncers are not guilded, but are essentially Tamol's private army.

Tamol is neither as tall nor as bulky as his brother, standing five feet six inches if he stretches. He does have Hamol's flaming red hair and fiery temper, and his reflexes are even faster than his brother's. People who do not know the brothers can easily mistake one for the other at a quick glance, realizing their mistake only after a long look or when they see the two men side by side.

Hamol and Tamol take turns to visit each other's taverns almost every night. They are quite friendly towards each other, sharing that special bond reserved for twins on any world or any plane of existence. They do compete for business, but neither brother would do anything to seriously or permanently damage his sibling's livelihood.

A well-kept secret between the brothers and Tamol's bouncers is the tunnel under Festival Street, which links the two taverns. It was dug secretly after Hamol took over the Wooden Leg, and runs between the cellars. It carefully avoids all sewers and other tunnels under the street. If a brawl erupts, or one of the brothers needs to move between the taverns unnoticed, the tunnel allows quick access between the cellars. In the confusion of an all-out brawl, no one notices where the bouncers come from, and they always return to the Rising Moon by walking across the street.

If a brawl erupts in the Moon, Hamol's hired Slayers are not sent to intervene. If Tamol's eight bouncers can't handle it, two more aren't going to help matters much.

Each tavern provides a general bulletin board where potential employers can post current jobs or out of work adventurers can make their availability known. There is no charge for using the board, since the brothers know they bring customers to the taverns. Almost all jobs involve guarding something, at least they claim to be. Even in Lankhmar, a notice seeking an able company to kidnap a city official would attract the attention of the city guards. The true natures of many jobs are revealed to adventurers only after they answer the notice. Then, they are committed to do the job, or they get hunted down and killed.

Adventure Hooks

There are several possibilities for starting adventures in either tavern.

First and most obvious, the party can answer an ad for some kind of guard duty. It might be work as caravan guards, or extra muscle on a ship heading into Mingol waters, or even a one night job acting as a deterrent at a noble's party. Payment for any of these jobs is by negotiation between the party and the hirer, but no more than one rilk per person per day should be paid, with possible bonuses if they are actually forced into combat.

Perhaps the PCs rent a room in one of the taverns and are to meet someone to discuss a job. In this case, the hirer has specifically sought out this band rather than take out a general ad, so the position of strength for negotiating a fee rests with the party. Still, no more than three smerduks per person per day should be paid unless the job is particularly hazardous or the party is of high level (average level 9th or above).

A little more esoteric an adventure hook is the possibility of one or more party members overhearing a plot to kidnap one of the Duchess Samara's grandchildren. They could do nothing, in which case the kidnap will happen, or they could alert the Duchess. In that case, once she has established that the threat is real and the PCs aren't the kidnapers themselves, she will reward them for the information and offer further rewards if they will stay and guard her estate until the attempt is made. Naturally, they must foil the attempt and neutralize the kidnapers by whatever means they deem necessary. The total reward for taking this assignment is 50 rilks per party member, plus an increase in social level among the Duchess and her social set.

Lastly, the setup of the taverns invites spying on others. As regular patrons, the party could be asked to catch a spy or even spy on other patrons.

CHAPTER 4

Adapting Adventures to Personal Campaigns

Most of the adventure hooks presented in this book are intended for low- to mid-level characters. Details for opponents have not generally been given to allow individual Dungeon Masters to tailor the adventures to suit the characters in their campaigns. Even high-level parties can be challenged by some of these adventures by increasing the number or toughness of the opponents. Treasure is also up to the DM, but remember to keep magical items to a bare minimum. Anything more powerful than a +1 weapon should be a major find (and often draws more trouble in its wake than it solves).

But what should the DM do if the adventure doesn't suit the campaign at all? Suppose your group dislikes doing work for hire, or their alignments, guild memberships, or religious beliefs conflict with the adventure. How do you get useful adventures and scenarios out of this book?

It's very simple—realize that there are always at least two sides to every story. Let's take a look back at some of the scenarios and explore other options.

Groups & Guilds

The Beggar's Guild: This particular group is always wary of outsiders looking for its secrets. A group of guild troubleshooters might have the job of weeding out spies in the organization. Any adventure in which city guards are killed has the possibility of bringing retribution on the perpetrators. Killing city guards and framing the PCs for the act is an excellent way of getting a party to leave Lankhmar to explore Nehwon.

The Charcoal Burners: The Overlord isn't the only one who wants to know about controlling the Deadly Smog. Any guild would give a lot for access to a means of eliminating competition and seizing power. Also, the Charcoal Burners know they don't have the ability, but they want outsiders to think they do. So, anyone asking too many questions needs to be silenced. This could be a job for the PCs, either as a limited job or as an ongoing contract with the guild.

The Embalmer's Guild: The player characters might be desperate for funds, and rather than be the guards of the fittings, they could be potential thieves. In this case, you should create NPC guards for the loot at a level suitable to your campaign.

The Taverners' Guild: The stolen ale is something everyone is after. Why should the party necessarily return it to its rightful owner? They might want to sell it to the highest bidder, or keep it themselves.

The Vermin Catchers: Rat God worshiping groups are not going to join the Vermin Catchers in a raid on Lankhmar Below. But, from the other perspective, they might easily join a raid by the rats on the guild house itself.

NPCs of Lankhmar

Angrew the Blacksmith: A blacksmith who can enchant his own works is dangerous to the status quo. Other blacksmiths are afraid of him and want him dead or run out of town. A client who has purchased a number of enchanted weapons wants to ensure their intended victim doesn't purchase enchanted weapons to defend himself. Black wizards might even wish him dead to keep themselves as the only sources of magical weaponry.

The Black Knight: This knight has annoyed a lot of people. There is no reason the PCs cannot be a hit squad for just about anyone, and kill the knight in a fair fight, or by some foul means. When her identity is revealed, her father will demand justice; this forces the PCs to become fugitives in yet another adventure-driven way to get them out of Lankhmar to other parts of Nehwon.

Calvin the Apothecary: Calvin is not immortal because of his magical potions. A sword can kill him as surely as it can kill any other human. Many of his secrets are written down, so intelligent people could replace Calvin, or keep his secrets just for themselves and maybe a few friends.

Charles the Inventor: Protecting Charles or obtaining his invention for their employer is not the only option. An aberrant party may wish to capture Charles' invention for its own use. Knowing other's thoughts is an enormous advantage in legal or illegal businesses. It is also a guaranteed way of screening out any spies and potential members whose interests or intentions are inimical to the PCs' interests.

Falesh the Fortune Teller: Many soothsayers are charlatans, or seem to be. Often this is because they do not wish to give a customer bad news, so they hedge around it. Some customers don't like being robbed, as they see it, and may want Falesh punished or exposed.

Fredoa: The suggested adventure with Fredoa has the PCs being checked out as possible recruits for Midnight's band. If none of them is even part-thief, they are rejected, but they can still perform the task of protecting Fredoa from harm. Or, they could secretly be working for the Thieves' Guild, or could sell information to the Thieves' Guild if they are approached to join Midnight's growing group.

Jermat and Martin: White and black wizards are sought out by two types of people—those who wish to buy their services, and those who only see them as a threat. Both Martin and Jermat could be visited by the PCs in either capacity.

Lamit the Storyteller: Suppose the PCs find Lamit's true identity and manage not to be killed by the Overlord's guards. What can they do with the information?

Sheldon: She doesn't want to be bothered by all those prying eyes. Since when did your band of adventurers care about one foreigner? Suppose that the PCs are worshipers of the Rat God and are working for the temple to find out why Sheldon hasn't been in yet? Now, instead of keeping others away from the lady, the PCs have to get around those who are trying to guard her privacy.

Whyseso the Minstrel: Whyseso could come to the attention of the Thieves' Guild and the PCs could well be on a mission to "invite" him to join the guild. The paranoid guild leaders could easily decide that Whyseso is their arch enemy, Midnight, and order the PCs to kill him.

Places of Interest in Lankhmar

The Cat O' Nines: The player characters could be clients of the Cat O' Nines, and have an interest in seeing that it isn't shut down by more scrupulous figures. They could become its defenders rather than its attackers.

The End Gate: This story presents two possibilities. What if the PCs were the disgraced guards who Redlock and his cohorts replaced? Might they not want their old jobs back and be prepared to do anything to get them? Redlock may be honest and incorruptible, but he can always be framed. . . .

The Haunted House: The advance guard of the ghouls is about the only story in this book that the characters cannot take either side on. If they live and work in Lankhmar, self-preservation should drive them to stop the ghouls, if they can.

The Squeaky Stoop: A female character suspects her husband or lover has been visiting the Squeaky Stoop behind her back and wishes the PCs to find out the truth for her. Rather than keeping spies away, the PCs could be the snoopers, looking for secret entrances so they can watch who comes and goes when the brothel reopens.

Some General Reminders

- Not much happens in Lankhmar without the involvement of the Thieves' Guild, or at least their knowledge.
- A party which double-crosses too many employers will soon gain a reputation for being untrustworthy. Such a reputation makes getting employment difficult. A double-crossing party will also invite retribution from their employers, and their victims as well.
- Cheating may be the normal thing in Lankhmar, but those cheated will usually want revenge and PCs are just as prone to assassinations and beatings as ordinary citizens. Remember that while cheating is chaotic behavior, it is not necessarily evil behavior.

JOIN THE RANKS OF THE FIGHTING ELITE!
NEW
Advanced Dungeons & Dragons 2nd Edition
The Complete PALADIN'S Handbook
Paladins – paragons of virtue, supreme champions of Good, and the noblest warriors of the AD&D® game. No matter how skilled or courageous, few fighters can aspire to this exalted status – only those who adhere to strict codes of behavior.
The Complete Paladin's Handbook details the unique requirements for creating these heroes and enhancing them with new proficiencies and equipment, new rules, and paladin kits like the skyrider, the inquisitor, and the indomitable wyrmslayer.
Don't miss this new Player's Handbook Rules Supplement available at book, game, and hobby stores everywhere!
TSR#2147 • Sug. Retail $18.00; CAN $23.00; £10.99 U.K. • ISBN 1-56076-845-2
® and ™ designate trademarks owned by TSR, Inc. ©1994 TSR, Inc. All Rights Reserved.